WICHITA NIMROD

WICHITA DETECTIVE
BOOK FIVE

PATRICK ANDREWS

ROUGH
EDGES
PRESS

Wichita Nimrod
Paperback Edition
Copyright © 2022 Patrick Andrews

Rough Edges Press
An Imprint of Wolfpack Publishing
9850 S. Maryland Parkway, Suite A-5 #323
Las Vegas, Nevada 89183

roughedgespress.com

Paperback ISBN 978-1-68549-187-1
eBook ISBN 978-1-68549-186-4
LCCN 2022948185

Dedicated to

Class of 1948
WILLARD ELEMENTARY SCHOOL
WICHITA, KANSAS

WICHITA NIMROD

"I know how terrible this is for you, dearest Dwayne. And I feel awful, too."

– Donna Sue Wheeler née Connors

CHAPTER 1

Newlyweds Dwayne Wheeler and his wife Donna Sue Wheeler née Connors returned to their private detective business after a brief honeymoon. They had gone on a car trip through the countryside in a planned itinerary that avoided cities in Kansas and Oklahoma. They wanted to enjoy the quiet, pleasant environments of small towns and the people living in them.

Now and then they pulled off bucolic roads to get out and stretch their legs. Dwayne, because of his illegal rumrunning in the past, didn't enjoy the sights as much as Donna Sue. She had lived all her life within the Wichita city limits. Now and then, a passing farmer would stop and ask if they needed any help. Dwayne always gave them a polite reply of, "No, sir. Ever'thing is just fine. But thanks for asking."

The couple also enjoyed stopping at eating places and having friendly chats with the locals. When Dwayne was asked what he did for a living, he stated he was a private detective. This brought about questions about his business and did he know the movie shamus Robert

Mitchum. This got to be irksome so Dwayne began saying he worked in a grocery store.

On the other hand, the two Wichitans were amazed how the locals seemed to know all about each other. Dwayne and Donna Sue listened to their conversations, as they exchanged bits of goings-on among themselves.

The only real drawback in the honeymoon was the lack of motor courts in the rural communities. When the couple wanted to end a day's driving, they headed for the state and U.S. highways.

After a couple of weeks of the honeymoon, the Wheelers were happy to return to Wichita.

———

A MONTH AFTER THEIR HOMECOMING THERE HAD been no capers for Dwayne to earn money. However, the large stash of secret cash they had hidden in the doorjamb of their bedroom closet took care of that situation. Since there were no clients, Dwayne wrote expenses made up for detective work. Donna Sue deposited the cash charged to those fraudulent compositions into their bank account. This would keep the Internal Revenue Service from discovering where their pseudo earnings were coming from.

Those slow days in the office always began in the mornings with Donna Sue phoning Millie at the Reliable Answering Service to see if there were any calls. With that unsuccessful task done, the couple would retire to the inner office to play cribbage at Dwayne's desk to pass the time.

Finally, on another quiet midmorning, Dwayne had just begun to shuffle the cards when the phone rang. Donna Sue picked up the handset and spoke her usual spiel. "Wheeler Detective Agency. Where may I direct your call?" After the caller gave Dwayne's name, she handed him the phone.

"Yeah?" the shamus said. "What can I do for you?"

"Hi, Dwayne. It's me, Harry Denver. How's things going?"

"Fine, Harry."

The caller, an old guy retired from the Wichita Police Department, was the house dick at the Riverview Hotel. "I want to see if you would be inter'sted in a temporary job here where I work."

"Sure. What's going on?"

"I gotta have a hernia operation," Harry explained. "I'll be gone for ten days or two weeks—something like 'at —I recommended you to the manager Charles Bentley to fill in for me. He said it'd be fine with him if you want the job."

"Mmm," Dwayne mused, recalling Bentley. "I thought he'd still be mad about Bernie Gordon and me beating up them Kansas City guys in the back alley of the hotel."

"Aw, naw! He understood what that was all about. And it kept them out-of-town hookers away. Bentley only wants girls from the Venus Services working here. They got class, y'know?"

"Most of 'em, I guess," Dwayne said. "Let's get back to the job. What are the hours I would be working?"

"It's a graveyard watch," Harry said, using police terminology. "Six p.m. to six a.m."

"And the pay?"

"I'm paid ten bucks a shift."

"Don't you get tips?"

"No. The bellboys have all the prospects for that. It's them that fetches the after-hours liquor and hookers.

They also carry suitcases for the guests and bring up room service and stuff like 'at. Lots and lots of tips."

"I tell you what, Harry. I'll have a talk with Bentley. If we can't work anything out, I'll fill in for you until somebody else can be found. Okay?"

"I appreciate that, Dwayne. Just don't ask him for too much, huh?"

Dwayne checked his watch. "I can go over there right now and see Bentley."

"If you work out a deal, I'll be on duty tonight and you can join me to see what the job is all about."

Dwayne hung up and looked over at Donna Sue. "Harry Denver the house dick at the Riverview is gonna have an operation for a hernia. He wants to know if I'll cover his job for a coupla weeks."

"You might as well," Donna opined. "What are you gonna charge the hotel?"

"Well...Harry gets ten bucks a shift."

"That's a lot less than the twenty-five a day you generally charge for your services."

"True," Dwayne remarked. "Harry didn't say so, but I know damn well if they can't get me to take his place, Charles Bentley will hire a permanent replacement. A Wichita Police pension ain't a hell of a lot. But I might get a little more dough than Harry since I ain't gonna be permanent."

"Take the job, Dwayne."

———

DWAYNE WALKED THROUGH THE HOTEL'S revolving doors to the front desk. The day receptionist Darrell Crawley looked up at his approach. "Hello, Dwayne. I know why you're here. I'll buzz Charles for you." He picked up a phone and pressed a button. "Dwayne Wheeler's here... okay." He hung up and motioned the shamus to come around the desk and go to the door marked MANAGER.

Dwayne knocked and stepped inside. "Hi, Charles. I hear you're gonna need a house dick."

The manager indicated a chair. "Sit down. I take it that Harry explained the situation to you."

"The basics of it, yeah. But I know you'll replace him permanently unless I take the job."

"I'd have to do that," the manager said. He cleared his throat. "The pay is ten dollars per shift."

"I'd like to get twelve."

Bentley shook his head. "Can't do it. It wouldn't make sense to pay you more than the guy that does the job permanently."

"Sure it would. If you hire a new replacement, you'll have to go through all sorts of paperwork and training. With me, you'll pay only twelve bucks cash off your books. That means no W-2 forms for the IRS."

"True."

"I'll need a shift with Harry to learn the routine. And I won't ask to be paid while he shows me around."

Charles Bentley drummed his fingers on the desktop for a moment of thought. Then he announced, "You're hired."

———

HARRY DENVER'S CUBBY HOLE OF AN OFFICE WAS on the first floor off to the side and behind the front desk. The next evening the night receptionist Paul Tracey and bellboy Jimmy Thompson gave Dwayne hellos as he walked up.

Jimmy was a slim, well-groomed kid in his early twenties and had been at the Riverview since dropping out of high school. He preferred working at night since that was the best time to get hookers and after-hours liquor for the guests. He had also helped Dwayne on a couple of capers that involved the hotel. He gave a salute to the shamus.

"Hi ya, Dwayne. It's good to see you."

"Good to see you, too, Jimmy."

"C'mon," the kid said. "I'll take you over to what Harry calls an office." He escorted Dwayne to the door and called out, "Are you in there, Harry?"

"Sure!"

Dwayne stepped inside and stopped to look around the small space. "Hey, Harry, it just dawned on me that I've never been in here before."

"Well, take a good gander. It ain't much but it's all mine."

The tiny room's furniture was made up of a desk, file cabinet, small bookcase, a couple of chairs and a cot with a thin mattress on it. It seemed depressing to Dwayne. It was all cheap and old in appearance. Kind of like Harry himself.

"Have a seat," the retired cop invited. "The first thing I want to do is thank you for taking the job. Charles told me you signed on for twelve bucks a shift and weren't gonna get paid for tonight's watch. That was real white of you, Dwayne. If you hadn't done me this favor, I'd've lost my job."

"Aw, hell, Harry. You and Jimmy helped me out a few times around here on a caper or two."

Harry stood up. "Well, let's begin the watch."

The house dick led the way out to the lobby. He signaled to Tracey the receptionist. "We're going for a look-around, Paul."

Harry avoided the elevator and went into the stairwell. "I always use the stairs unless I got a reason to go to a certain floor because of an emergency. We got eight floors here and I walk up and back three times each shift."

"Christ! No wonder you got a hernia, Harry!"

"Prob'ly. By the way, don't go no place away from the office without letting Tracey know where you're going. That's a hard and fast rule"

"Gotcha," Dwayne said.

"There's house phones on ever' floor if you need to contact the desk."

"Gotcha," Dwayne repeated.

"The second floor has all the fancy suites. The eighth is for offices and businesses."

Harry continued the tour, informing him that the rooms from the third floor up to the seventh had transoms. "Sometimes a guest needs to be spied on. I got step ladders in the housekeeping closets to check such things out."

The tour continued as Harry explained the other requirements of the job.

CHAPTER 2

Dwayne's work at the Riverside Hotel was slow and boring for the first three nights. Between taking walks throughout the building, he sat in Harry's office with his feet up on the desk, chain-smoking his preferred Lucky Strike cigarettes. He also snuck into the closed kitchen to scrounge goodies out of the cabinets and refrigerators.

He envied the bellboy Jimmy Thompson. The kid was busy at the bell captain's desk taking requests for hookers or liquor. He was also summoned up to rooms to straighten out small problems for the guests such as bringing towels and newspapers. When the requested alcohol or prostitutes showed up in the alley behind the hotel, a buzz sounded on the bell captain's desk. Jimmy then answered the summons to either escort a call girl or carry booze up to the appropriate client. Either way, he was given large tips.

IT WAS WELL INTO THE FOURTH NIGHT AND Dwayne was playing solitaire in Harry's office when he heard the phone ring out at the front desk. Paul Tracey the receptionist answered, "Front desk. How may I serve you?...I see...loud radio in Room 404...you are across the hall in 405. I'll send the hotel's detective to deal with the problem." He hung up and called out, "Dwayne!"

"I heard you, Paul," the shamus said. "I'm on my way."

He had learned how to operate the elevator during other capers at the hotel. He had no desire to climb stairs like Harry. In less than a minute he brought the conveyance to a stop and pushed the door open. Dwayne walked out into the hall looking for Room 405. He could hear the loud radio coming from Room 404. He knocked on 405 and a grumpy man who had made the complaint opened the door. "Do you hear that son of a bitch?" he asked.

"That's what I'm here for, sir. I'll take care of this right away."

Dwayne walked across the hall and hammered on the door with his closed fist. "Open up!" He banged it a few more times.

A trio of other guests stuck their heads out into the hall to see what was going on. One, a middle-age lady, said, "Thank heavens! That radio is keeping me awake!"

The other two also expressed their displeasure about the situation.

Dwayne gave up knocking and went down the hall to the housekeeping closet. He pulled out a stepladder. He mounted it and looked through the transom. An extremely fat man was lying on his back with the radio blaring from the nightstand.

"Hey!" Dwayne yelled. "Hey! Hey! Hey!"

He got no reaction so he stepped down and pulled out the passkey from his jacket pocket. He opened the door and stepped inside, going to the radio and turning it off. He shook the snoring, sleeping man hard.

The guy made blubbery noises through his thick lips, then opened his eyes. "Huh?" He looked at the nightstand. "Who turned off my radio?"

"I did. There's been complaints about you playing it too loud."

"Who the hell are you?"

"I'm the hotel detective. I could hear it all the way down the hall when I stepped out of the elevator."

"That's the only way I can sleep," the fat man stated. He reached over and turned the radio back on.

Dwayne turned it off then unplugged the instrument and picked it up. "I'm taking this out of the room."

"You better not! I'll report you!"

Dwayne ignored the threat, and headed for the door. The fat man, wearing a nightshirt, got off the bed and followed the departing shamus into the hall. He hit him between the shoulder blades. There wasn't much force behind the blow but it caused Dwayne to drop the radio. He spun around, and in doing so, scared the fat man into waddling backward to avoid getting punched.

Dwayne was angry enough to beat the guy up, but he knew if he did, he would be replaced by a new hotel detective and Harry Denver would lose his job. Anyway the guy wasn't going to make a fistfight out of the incident.

The three guests clapped their hands and called out thanks. Dwayne growled at the fat man. "Get outta this hall. Now! *Now!*"

"I'm gonna report you!" fatty said, hurrying back inside his room.

Dwayne replaced the stepladder then walked to the

elevator and went down to the lobby and approached the front desk. Paul Tracey had a worried expression on his face. "That guy in Room 404 just called down and said you attacked him."

"I'm the one that got hit. And I didn't even throw one punch at him."

"Well, you'd better stay around in the morning until Charles Bentley comes in. He's going to want to get the lowdown on the fight."

"There wasn't a fight, goddamn it!" Dwayne snarled.

"This is serious, Dwayne. There could be a lawsuit."

Dwayne carried the radio into the detective office and sat down to fume and worry. He had really fucked things up for Harry.

———

DWAYNE WAITED UNTIL CHARLES BENTLEY CAME in at seven o'clock. After Paul told the manager about the previous night's incident, he and the shamus went into his office. Bentley was livid as he glared at Dwayne.

"What the hell came over you? Surely you're aware of the law! You can't go around hitting the guests! You should have dealt with him in a polite, careful manner and solved the problem like a civilized man. You could always call the cops if the situation got real serious. The hotel is going to get sued! A new house detective will have to be hired. That means Harry Denver is out of a job."

Dwayne was about to say he never punched the man, but was interrupted when the day receptionist Darrell Crawley stepped into the office. "Excuse me."

Bentley looked over at him. "We're busy, Darrell."

"This concerns last night's problem," Darrell said.

"There are three people here that expressed their appreciation of how Dwayne handled the disturbance."

"Wait here," Bentley ordered the shamus. He followed Darrel out to the front desk. Ten minutes later there was a smile on his face when he returned. "I just got the whole story. And they say the obese man hit you from behind and you did not strike him. If this comes to a lawsuit we have those guests' home addresses to back us up in court. But I don't think that will be a problem. Paul said the guy that played the radio so loud had checked out an hour ago." He walked over and offered his hand to Dwayne. "You proved you're a real professional."

"Glad to be of service," Dwayne growled. "I'm going home now."

———

THE REST OF DWAYNE'S STINT AT THE Riverview was what would be expected. There were long hours of absolute boredom, but every once in a while a minor disturbance occurred.

An inebriated husband and wife walked into the lobby two evenings after the radio incident. It was evident they had been doing some serious pub crawling. They began a shouting match over the woman's behavior toward a man in one of the taverns they had been in. Dwayne and Jimmy walked over and ushered them into the elevator. After reaching the third floor where the couple's room was located, Dwayne had calmed them down enough to avoid further disturbance.

Another bit of trouble settled.

———

THE NEXT EVENING AT TEN O'CLOCK, A YOUNG woman came in through the revolving doors and approached Paul Tracey at the front desk. It was obvious she had seen better days. There were rents in her nylons, her clothing was cheap and had obviously been worn for quite a while. Her legs needed shaved and clearly she was tired and scared.

Paul the desk clerk was somewhat confused. "Yes?"

"I'd like to entertain some johns."

"I can't help you, miss. However, I can get our house dick to explain our...er, our... curriculum on that subject." He walked over to the detective office and rapped on the door. "Dwayne!"

Dwayne set down the copy of *Esquire* magazine he was reading. "What?"

Paul opened the door. "There's a hooker out here. It's obvious she isn't from Venus Services."

"Send her in."

When the young woman appeared, Dwayne saw she was the quintessential hard-luck gal. He motioned to the chair in front of the desk. "Have a seat, Miss."

The woman was nervous and afraid, but Dwayne's friendly manner calmed her somewhat. She cleared her throat. "I'd like to turn some tricks in this hotel."

"Well, we already have a service for call girls."

"Oh. Then I would like to join it."

Dwayne didn't want to hurt her feelings about not being attractive or chic enough, so he tried to be as diplomatic as he could. "Oh, gosh! There ain't any openings right now. And there's a...well...a pretty long waiting list."

"I would kick back half of what I earned to you."

Dwayne shrugged, recognizing it was time for a white lie. "What's your name?"

"Maybelle."

"Okay, Maybelle. I'll put you on the list. But it'll be a long, long time before you are called. Prob'ly a couple of years."

"What about just tonight," she begged. "I really need some money. I just got into Wichita. I saw this hotel and hoped I could service some nice gentlemen."

"D'you have a pimp or a husband?"

"I got a boyfriend but he ran away after he dropped me off in Wichita. A cop saw me on the street and took me to the Transit Lodgings where I can stay for free. They'll only let me sleep there for three nights then I gotta leave. I ain't got a dime!"

Dwayne shook his head. "I'm really sorry."

"I'll give you a blow job for a dollar."

He shook his head.

"Fifty cents!"

Dwayne reached into his back pocket and pulled out his wallet. He took all the bills in it. "Take this. And leave the Transit Lodgings tomorrow morning. Go to the Salvation Army. It's a couple of blocks farther down the street from where you're staying now. You'll get some real help. They can even find you work. Honest work."

The young woman stared in disbelief at the money. She began to sob as she picked it up. "This is fifteen bucks, sir!"

Dwayne, who hadn't known how much he had in his wallet, shrugged. "Yeah. Sure. Fifteen bucks." He was too proud to take back the money.

Maybelle broke out crying. "This is the first kindness showed me in a long time, Mister...I don't even know your name."

They were interrupted by Jimmy sticking his head in the door. "Hey, Dwayne. I got to make a liquor run. You want anything?"

"No. But how about giving Maybelle here a ride down to the Transit Lodgings."

"Sure. I'd be glad to."

Maybelle gave Dwayne Wheeler a look of sincere gratitude.

The shamus was deeply thoughtful after the unfortunate young woman left with the bellboy. Her desperate and fearful straits reminded him of a bizarre undercover F.B.I. caper he had been on months before. He and a G-man by the name of Terry McCarthy had been assigned to infiltrate a gang war among Irish thugs, a Sicilian mob and two different Mafia families in the middle of the Kansas prairie. Powerful criminal operations from the east coast had moved into the rural area for unknown reasons. The Feds wanted to find out what was going on, and enlisted Dwayne as an undercover operative to back up McCarthy. The investigation included prostitutes who worked the truck stops. Like Maybelle, the women weren't exactly in the elite of whoredom.

His recollections suddenly cast his mind into several horrible incidents that had occurred in that off-the-wall assignment. The first was when the leader of the gang he had infiltrated gave him orders to kill a member of one of the rival crime organizations. The target was a mafioso by the name of Fat Pauly Cappurio. The shamus had never killed another human being, but he had no choice in the matter. If he failed or refused the assignment he would not only expose the F.B.I. sting, he would be shot dead by his gang boss. McCarthy volunteered to go with him. He recognized Dwayne's hesitation and reminded him that Fat Pauly was a public enemy and a murderer himself. "Killing the son of a bitch will rid the world of a useless mad dog."

"I still don't like having to do it."

The hit occurred in the parking area of a truck stop. Ten minutes of fretful waiting passed before the approach of the victim could be heard on the gravel around the trucks. When Fat Pauly came into view, Dwayne stepped out from behind an eighteen-wheeler and aimed the pistol at his target. He pulled the trigger with the muzzle inches from the gangster's head. The silencer on the weapon allowed only a "pop" sound. With that done, he and McCarthy quickly withdrew.

Dwayne had never told Donna Sue about the killing. Now, fretting about the past in the hotel detective office, he wished he'd ordered Jimmy to pick him up a pint of Jack Daniel's Sour Mash Whisky on his liquor run.

CHAPTER 3

In Reno County, Kansas, a dilapidated old farm house sat at a crossroads in an out-of-the-way location. The dwelling had been built more than sixty years previously by an Irish carpenter by the name of Dennis Gilhooly. He had helped local homesteaders in the area meet U.S. Government regulations that required permanent houses to be erected on their claims. Gilhooly was not a homesteader, but his carpentry skills earned him enough money to purchase a small plot of land outside the settlements.

The house he built was a sturdy two-story structure. The bottom floor was a parlor and kitchen. The upstairs consisted of six small rooms for bedrooms or storage. Gilhooly eventually married a local woman who, unfortunately, died in childbirth. The baby boy survived and was christened Timothy. He grew to manhood and wed Lilly Johnson, a farmer's daughter. They had four children—three sons and a daughter—who all grew to adulthood. By then Dennis Gilhooly had died and was buried on the property.

Timothy, however, was neither a good father nor

provider, and deserted the family. He wandered into Kentucky where he became a professional gunman for an organization that provided scabs during coalmine strikes. One particularly violent clash between management and labor ended up with him being shot dead by an enraged picketer.

Lilly and her children never received any news of Tim's demise.

———

BY THE 1940S, LILLY STILL LIVED IN THE HOUSE with her three sons, Junior 24, Cornelius 22 and Horatio 18. Junior's real name was Timothy Gilhooly, Jr., but the family always called him Junior. This was because Lilly did not want her missing husband's name to be mentioned—ever!

However, another member of the family had deserted the residence and disappeared. This was a 20-year-old daughter called Sister. After the girl had run away, she was never mentioned among the mother and the siblings. "If she don't love us, then we don't love her," Lilly pronounced. And whatever their mother proclaimed, the compliant siblings agreed with those opinions.

The two elder brothers had grown up to be heavily muscled with bushy caterpillar eyebrows over dull eyes. They had served sentences in the Kansas State Penitentiary for burglary. Horatio, as the youngest, was his mother's darling. He was much better looking than his older siblings and he had never been in trouble with the law. Lilly had decided to keep him in the house and out of school. Kansas laws allowed students to quit their education after completing the 8th grade. Horatio had been a straight "A" student and was devastated by having to give up his studies.

Their home still didn't have electricity or running water after the passage of more than sixty years. However, a cistern was located next to the rear of the house for an ample water supply. This was drawn up from the small reservoir via a hand pump. The toilet was an outhouse five yards from the dwelling. The Gilhoolys had enough sense to put it in a proper spot where its contents did not drain into or around the cistern.

The house itself was in extremely bad shape because the current inhabitants never had enough money to keep it in good repair. The roof leaked badly, but pots and pans caught the drips. Scrounged plywood replaced broken windowpanes and rattled on windy days and nights.

———

ONE CLOUDY PRAIRIE DAY, AFTER A RATHER sparse breakfast of bread and syrup, Lilly called a family meeting. This was an occasional custom that the ever obedient boys observed as they sat around the kitchen table to hear what she had to say.

Lilly, with a square jaw under a flat nose, announced. "We got some serious things to consider here this morning. Our money jar is just about empty and so is our larder. That means we're gonna have to get us some more greenbacks."

Junior spoke up. "There ain't no sense in us looking for jobs, Ma. Nobody around here will hire us."

Cornelius moaned. "That's 'cause me and Junior ended up doing three years in the penitentiary."

"I've took that into consideration," Lilly informed him. "I ain't talking about stealing from junk yards and construction places. My new idea is not only gonna get us more money but is safer, too." She gave them a crooked grin. "Now tell me what's special about Sunday mornings."

The boys exchanged puzzled glances, then turned their attention back to their mother for the answer.

Lilly continued, "That's when just about ever' farm family goes to church. And I learned something real important during that summer I was cooking for a harvest crew. D'you know what that is?"

Again there was mutual silence.

Lilly was exasperated. "While them farmers is gone to church they don't lock their doors. In fact, they don't never lock their doors. Them people don't have to worry about getting robbed. And on Sunday all are out of their houses leaving the doors wide open."

More masculine silence.

Lilly lost her temper. "Are you three really that thick between your goddamn ears? Let me explain. If they're away from home at church and the doors to their houses ain't locked—"

"—we can just walk inside!" Horatio interrupted.

"Right!" Lilly happily sang out. "As always my youngest is the brightest."

Her mood plummeted when Junior then inquired, "So what do we do in them houses, Ma?"

"Are you that thick-headed!" Lilly shouted. "You *steal* stuff! And we sell it to Shorty Barlow like we always did with the other stuff we stole. But this time we can peddle clothes, kitchen stuff, guns, bullets and other things like 'at."

Cornelius had a question. "What about the farmers' dogs, Ma? They don't go to church and we could get bit."

"There's them bullets and pistols hanging in our front closet."

"That's right," Junior said. "We got two Colt Detective snub-nose pistols and waist holsters to hold 'em."

"So you just shoot any frisky dog that wants to bite" Lilly stated. "And them farmers ain't gonna hear the shots since they'll be in church singing and praying and making all sorts of noises."

Horatio spoke up. "May I carry a gun, Ma?"

"No, sweetie. Your brothers know how to handle 'em. And you don't." She looked at the others. "Now here's some reminders for you. We leave Reno County completely alone. This is where we live. And also Sedgwick County is where Wichita is. There's too many folks living there and they all got sense enough to lock their doors when they go somewhere."

"Where are we gonna start, Ma?" Cornelius asked.

"We're gonna begin in Kingman County. We'll only rob two homes for each county each Sunday. That'll keep the sheriffs from thinking they got a crime wave on their hands." She paused and gave them a stern look. "Now let's start getting things ready. First thing is gloves so you don't leave fingerprints. The next thing is to put gas in the car. After that I'll pick out where you to go to do the stealing. You can start this coming Sunday."

"Yes, Ma," they spoke in unison.

———

A WEEK HAD GONE BY SINCE HARRY DENVER HAD been released from the hospital and returned to his job at the Riverview Hotel. Dwayne was once more going with Donna Sue to their office.

During this time, he was called to go on two

capers. A businessman wanted Dwayne to follow his partner for a couple of weeks to see where he went during the day when he made sales calls. The client didn't say so, but Dwayne knew he was worried that the guy was seeing his wife. The second job he had was in one of the downtown department stores to check employees who might be stealing merchandise. Both assignments turned out positive, relieving the worries of his clients, and earning the shamus some big bucks.

———

ON A MONDAY MORNING AFTER A RELAXING weekend, Donna Sue had just finished checking in with Millie at the Reliable Answering Service while Dwayne wrote up fake caper reports in order to launder more cash money into the bank account.

Donna Sue got up from her desk and walked back to see how Dwayne was doing. She read over his shoulder as he scribbled down phony reports. She reminded him to not be too unrealistic, then went back to the front section of the office.

Just as she sat down a frail rapping sounded on the door. "Come in," Donna Sue invited.

A young woman wearing cheap clothing that included a very uncomplimentary hat with an artificial flower pinned on one side, stepped in. "I would like to speak to Mister Wheeler please."

Donna Sue raised her voice. "Dwayne! There's someone here to see you."

When Dwayne appeared, he broke into a grin. "Maybelle, how'd you know where to find me?"

"I went to the hotel and a feller at the big desk told me

where you had an office." She reached into her purse and pulled out two dollars. "Here."

"What's this for?"

"For the fifteen dollars you gimme. I can pay you off two dollars a week. And I follered your advice and left the Transit Lodgings and went to the Salvation Army. You was right about them. They got me a room in a hotel. And I can stay there as long as I need to."

"Yeah," Dwayne said. "The Salvation Army was very kind to me and my mother a long time ago."

Maybelle continued, "They got me a job in a laundry close by."

"I'm happy for you, Maybelle. And I want you to consider the fifteen dollars a gift. You don't have to pay me anything."

"But I want to, Mister Wheeler!"

He walked over to Maybelle and took her by the arm, steering her toward the door. "Now you just forget about that. And get on with your life, Maybelle. I know this is your first step toward genuine happiness."

She stood on her toes and kissed his cheek. "Thank you ever so much, Mister Wheeler. You're a kind man."

She walked out the door and Donna Sue turned to Dwayne. "What was that all about?"

"I met Maybelle at the Riverview while I was standing in for Harry Denver. One night she showed up wanting to work as a whore. She told me about not having any money and her boyfriend leaving her in the lurch. She offered to give me a blow job."

Donna Sue snapped, "And you paid her fifteen dollars for a blowjob?"

"No! I *gave* her fifteen bucks because that was all I had in my wallet. I wanted to help her. Didn't you hear what she said about paying me back?"

Donna Sue sat down, her face blushing with embarrassment. "I'm sorry, sweetie. I should have known. That was an awful way I acted toward the poor girl."

Dwayne turned to go back in his office. "For crying out loud! I'd never pay fifteen dollars for a blow job!"

Donna Sue gave him a fierce frown. "Just how much would you pay for one?"

Dwayne realized she didn't think the joke was funny. "I don't know...I mean I wouldn't...that is—"

"Just stay on the straight and narrow," Donna Sue warned him. She settled back in her chair and gave the girl some thought. There was some comeliness deep down in that unfortunate young woman.

CHAPTER 4

The Gilhooly family car was a blue 1927 Model A Ford. They had actually bought it legally from a farm family on the east side of Reno County. It was their late grandfather's favorite vehicle, but none of his descendants had any desire for it.

One positive thing about the two older Gilhooly boys was that deep within their befuddled intellects were flashes of expertness when it came to automobiles. They kept the old engine in good shape, the brakes in working order and the radiator cool. The young men also covered the ancient vehicle with a tarpaulin when it was parked under the cottonwood tree in front of the house. This latter task was to keep the messy cotton seedpods from the tree limbs from falling and sticking to the car.

——

Now, early on a cloudy Sunday morning, the three Gilhooly lads were going down a rural road in Kingman County, with Junior driving the Model A. He and Cornelius had the snub-nose revolvers in their waist holsters in case of unfriendly dogs. The brothers all looked out the car's windows for any nearby farm houses. They came to a dusty intersection and stopped.

Junior ordered, "Corny, take a look around."

Cornelius got out of the car, dragging a wooden kitchen stool with him. He climbed up on it and scanned the area.

"Hey! Over to the right. There's a house. Let's check it out."

Junior waited until both brother and stool were back in the car, then stepped on the gas. They went down a quarter of a mile to the farmhouse and Junior stopped. They all gave the yard and driveway a close, careful study.

"There isn't a car," young Horatio announced. "That means those people are at church."

Junior put the Model A in gear and drove up to a side door of the house and parked. "Let's go, boys."

The trio walked up to the door and tried the knob. The entry opened and they went inside. "Let's not waste time!" Junior ordered.

Cornelius and Horatio went through the house, pulling out drawers and looking into closets. Meanwhile Junior scoured the kitchen for cooking implements. He found an empty coffee can with greenbacks and coins. He picked it up along with an old fashion iron skillet, a Sunbeam Mixmaster and a Sunbeam Coffeemaster. He held it all in his arms, and called out, "You guys got anything?"

The two came into the kitchen. Cornelius had an old Winchester .30-.30 carbine while Horatio carried a 12-guage pump-action Remington shotgun. They quickly left the house and put the loot in the car's luggage trunk.

"We'll hit one more place then head for home," Junior said. "Just like Ma told us to do."

———

Tommy Brady was Dwayne's best friend despite the difference in their ages. He and his late wife Margie had retired from the Wichita Salvation Army organization and lived on the farm Margie's parents had left her. The property was located outside the small town of Augusta. However, rather than doing any agriculture work themselves, the couple rented out the land to various local farmers.

When they first met, Tommy had been a boatswain's mate in the navy and held the Pacific Fleet's middleweight boxing championship. He was a tough little guy, profane and short-tempered. When he wasn't knocking opponents out in the ring, he brawled in saloons from the China Sea to the South Pacific.

One memorable evening in 1925 when his ship was in San Francisco he went on shore leave to look for some raucous recreation. True to form, he headed for the roughest part of the waterfront for his three favorite pastimes; whoring, drinking and brawling. As he swaggered toward his preferred hangouts, he sighted a Salvation Army band playing on a street corner. Normally he would have passed by without giving the group as much as a second glance. But one of the young ladies playing a clarinet caught his eye. She was cute and her eyes had a glow that made Tommy's Irish heart come to a complete stop.

Sure and she's an angel on earth, he thought to himself.

The sailor dropped some money in the pot set in

front of the band. Everyone, including the charming clarinet player, nodded their thanks to him and continued the performance. He started off toward his original destination, but abruptly turned around to retrace his steps back to the musicians.

A series of events occurred that same evening after Tommy volunteered to help the band take their instruments back to the Salvation Army headquarters. He began an acquaintanceship with Miss Margie Thompson the clarinetist, and visited the Salvation Army Center on every shore leave after that.

As time passed, the couple fell in love. It was under Margie's influence and affection that Tommy changed his wild ways and did not reenlist when his hitch in the Navy was up. He became an employee of the Salvation Army, and was provided with a small room. The former sailor began attending all the religious services on Sunday mornings and Wednesday evenings. He proposed to Margie and she accepted. Eventually he joined the Salvation Army proper.

As the couple drew closer to retirement, Margie decided that they should leave San Francisco and transfer to the Salvation Army in Wichita. That way they could be near her family's farm when it was time for their retirement. After three years in Wichita the couple retired and moved onto the farm. It was a happy time for both until Margie suffered a stroke. She became bedridden and died from a cardiac arrest three months later.

A grief-stricken Tommy was left alone.

———

TOMMY BRADY WAS IN A HURRY AS HE DROVE HIS pickup truck toward his farm after the morning services at the Methodist church in Augusta. Dwayne and Donna Sue had invited him to a lunch in Wichita at the downtown Continental Grill. He was looking forward to the meal for three personal reasons: the first was because of his affection for Dwayne and Donna Sue; the second because the restaurant was his favorite; and the third because they were going to drive out to his farm and pick him up as well as bring him back.

When Tommy turned off the road and headed toward his house, he saw Dwayne's Nash station wagon parked off to the side of the yard. He honked his horn twice as he braked to a stop. Dwayne and Donna Sue stepped through the kitchen door onto the small wooden back stoop.

The shamus called out, "Hey, Tommy! You ready to eat at the good ol' Continental Grill?"

Tommy laughed as he walked toward the house with a Bible under his arm. "I can already hear a hamburger and French fries calling me."

"Hi, Tommy," Donna Sue said. She kissed him on the cheek. "How've you been?"

"Fit as a fiddle. How about you two?"

Dwayne answered, "Business is good."

Tommy patted Dwayne on the shoulder. "Let's go into the house while I freshen up; if you know what I mean." He led the others inside and laid his Bible on the kitchen table. "I'll only be a moment."

A few minutes later the three were going west on U.S. Highway 54. It quickly turned into Kellogg Street once they crossed the city limits. After entering the downtown area, Dwayne easily found a parking place. The inner-city neighborhood was always empty on Sundays when all the stores were closed.

When the trio entered the restaurant, they walked

down a row of booths along the wall. A waitress quickly appeared to take their orders. Tommy asked for a hamburger, French fries and coffee; Donna Sue requested a club sandwich, potato chips and ice tea; Dwayne ordered a grilled cheese sandwich, French fries and an Orange Crush. That was his favorite meal.

"Well!" Donna Sue said after the waitress left to fill the orders. "Let's bring ourselves up-to-date while we wait for the food. You first, Tommy."

He shrugged. "Same ol' stuff, I guess. Now and then I drive over to the Chatterbox Diner on Highway 54 to escape my own cooking." He suddenly remembered something. "Hey!" he said to Dwayne, "wasn't that the place where you went when that bootlegger was killed?"

"Yeah," Dwayne replied. "That was during the caper when the Kansas City mob was trying to move into Wichita. There was a shootout and Mack Crofton was killed. I'll always regret that since I talked him into helping me out."

"You can't blame yourself, Dwayne," Tommy said.

"Well...let's talk about something else."

Donna Sue turned to Dwayne. "Tell Tommy about that girl."

"What girl?"

"You know! The one that visited you while you were working at the Riverview."

Tommy laughed out loud. "Have you been earning money as a bellboy, Dwayne?"

Dwayne chuckled. "No. I was covering for the hotel detective who was gonna have an operation. And this young girl by the name of Maybelle came in and wanted to entertain male guests that desired feminine company, if you get my drift."

"I understand."

Dwayne continued, "She wasn't very pretty and looked wore out."

Donna Sue spoke up. "There's a certain beauty down deep in that young girl. I'm sure of it."

"Prob'ly," Dwayne agreed. "Anyhow I told her the call girls that came there were from a group that had a waiting list. Maybelle begged me to let her work there at least for two or three johns. She said she was staying at the Transit Lodgings and could only be there for three nights."

Tommy said, "That place does the best they can. Unpaid volunteers run it and they get gifts and money from local churches."

"Anyhow," Dwayne continued, "I gave her some money—"

Donna Sue interrupted. "Tommy, he pulled every bill he had from his wallet and gave it to her. Fifteen dollars!"

"That was kind of you, Dwayne."

"I told Maybelle about the Salvation Army and she ended up with a room at the Randall Hotel."

"Oh, yeah," Tommy said. "The Wichita Salvation Army has used that place for decades. It's clean and safe."

"I know," Dwayne said. "That's where you guys put me and my mom."

"I remember that well."

"Anyhow, they got her a job at the Whitaker Laundry. That was what my mom did, too."

Tommy smiled. "Well, you got a good mark up there in the Golden Book of Heaven, Dwayne."

They were interrupted when the waitress showed up with their orders. The young woman expertly balanced a tray as she laid out the food and drinks. "Can I get you anything else?"

"No thanks," Donna Sue said.

The waitress walked away and the three people settled

down to eat and speak of things that had nothing to do with shootouts, poor women prostituting themselves or Dwayne's mother working hard in a laundry before she died of cancer.

Their conversation was made up of the more pleasant times of the past.

Chapter 5

Shorty Barlow was a rural entrepreneur who had a shabby second-hand business near a country crossroad southeast of Hutchinson, Kansas. Shorty was five feet, six inches tall, obese, unshaven and always had a chaw of tobacco in the left side of his wide mouth. He wore denim shirts and bib overalls every day. In the winter he added a mackinaw jacket to his bucolic raiment to keep out the cold.

Because of long past carelessness that occurred during periods of wild drunken binges, he was married to two women at the same time. One in Oklahoma and another in Texas. This was why he lived and worked in Kansas.

Shorty bought, sold and bartered a myriad of merchandise. However, his main trade was in auto and truck parts he purchased from chop shops that dismantled stolen motor vehicles.

His enterprise was located within a barbed wire enclosure that surrounded a warehouse and a house. A gasoline-driven generator and well pump provided the sanitation as did the septic tank in the back of the dwelling.

The site could be reached by turning off the junction and driving down a narrow trail, crossing a creek on a rickety bridge and finally turning off the road to go between two windbreaker columns of trees. There, flanked by the rows of elms, was where Shorty conducted his less than respectable dealings.

Trading, buying, selling and bartering were Shorty's inborn talents. And he gave his clients—both the buyers and sellers—fair prices when dealing. He knew the wares brought to him were not legally obtained. Therefore, he had placed a crude sign over the counter in the store which read:

DONT TELL ME NOTHIN AND I WONT SAY NOTHIN

Shorty Barlow was a wealthy man who kept no books, used no banks and hid his cash money. And he did not advertise his business, paid no taxes, didn't use a telephone, never possessed a birth certificate; and had no close kin that he knew of. This meant that nobody, outside of a few people, were aware of his existence on this earth.

He did have a staff of sorts. Jeb and Katy Clemens, a couple he had met in Oklahoma, were in their early forties and most happy to be in his employment. Jeb was a tall, muscular man who spoke softly and demonstrated a true love for Katy. His duty was to pick up and deliver the material Shorty needed to keep his business solvent. Jeb drove a weather-beaten 1936 Ford panel truck to take care of his chores. Also, when an occasional argument arose during bargaining with an angry customer, he would step in between Shorty and the complainant to make sure the boss was protected. Jeb had a Kansas driver's license he kept up to date. That way he didn't have to worry if he was pulled over by the law.

His wife Katy was a serious, plump woman with red hair and freckles. She was the cook, housekeeper and laundress of the organization. She was the reason the crude buildings, so weatherworn on the outside, were clean and well-kept on the inside. Katy was also an expert with the pedal-driven Singer sewing machine belonging to her and Jeb.

———

JUNIOR GILHOOLY, WITH HIS MOTHER LILLY beside him, drove across the bridge that led to the rows of windbreaker trees around Shorty's store. Cornelius and Horatio sat in the backseat.

Junior went through the open gate in the barbed wire fence and parked in front of the warehouse. Lilly struggled out of the car and led her brood over to the entrance of the building.

Shorty, examining the most recent acquisition of automobile parts with Jeb, looked up at the Gilhoolys' arrival. He grinned so wide that his tobacco-stained teeth were visible in all their yellow and brown glory.

He greeted, "How do, Miz Gilhooly. What can I do for you?"

"I got some extry stuff that I'd like to be rid of."

"Why sure!" Shorty happily acknowledged. "Drive your car around to the back and we'll see what I can do for you." He glanced at the three boys. "Howdy, fellers. How's things going?"

Junior, ever the spokesman, reported. "Real good, Mister Barlow."

Shorty stepped out the rear door and walked up to the Gilhooly car. Junior opened the luggage rack and began pulling out the loot. The first were ten assorted firearms. Shorty checked each one. "These have all been well kept, Miz Gilhooly," he said. "But, as you prob'ly remember, I don't pay much for 'em since there's a hell of a lot of guns out there." He thought a moment, then announced, "I'll give you ten bucks for all of 'em."

Junior and Horatio unloaded some kitchen appliances. There was a two dozen assortment of coffeemakers, mixers, electric skillets and choppers. Shorty's eyes opened wide with approval. He checked everything. "Twenty bucks."

The next presentation was women's and children's clothing that had been pulled off closet racks of the farmhouses. All were in good shape, clean and ironed. Among them was garb for both men and women, clothes for children from toddlers to teenagers, and a variety of hats and work clothing.

Shorty inspected the clothes. "I can't take the overalls and all that work stuff. I'm afraid that Sears Roebucks and Montgomery Ward catalogs has me beat on prices."

There were also bags of dirty laundry the brothers had picked up in a couple of places. Horatio dumped them out on the ground. Shorty sorted through them. "These is real good, Miz Gilhooly. I can get Katy to wash and iron 'em. I'll give you ten bucks for all them duds."

Ma Gilhooly was satisfied. "I'll take it, Mister Barlow."

Shorty reached into a pocket on his bib overalls and retrieved his wallet. He counted out forty dollars. "Nice doing business with nice folks," he intoned.

"Is Katy around?" Lilly asked.

"She's at the house," he answered, and turned toward

the warehouse, hollering, "Jeb! C'mon back here and help me carry in this load."

Lilly sent the boys to the car, then walked over to the house door and knocked. Katy answered, "Come on in!"

Lilly stepped inside and saw Katy working at the pedal-driven Singer sewing machine. "Howdy, Katy. I just brung in some stuff and sold it to Shorty."

"Well, I'm glad you stopped by," Katy said. She got up and walked over to a cabinet. "Are you ready for a snort or two?"

"You betcha!"

Katy fetched two glasses and a pint bottle of rye whisky, and led the way to the kitchen table. "Sit down there and let's palaver."

Lilly took two big swallows of the strong liquor. "Whew! That was a kicker."

Katy did the same. "I reckon you've had them boys of yours out doing some shopping." She knew well that they stole merchandise, but never mentioned it aloud.

"Yeah. We picked up some goods. Guns, clothes and kitchen stuff."

"Shorty likes them new-fangled automatic mixers and coffeemakers."

Lilly agreed. "You can say that again." She glanced at the sewing machine. "Whatcha doing?"

"I'm mending some of Jeb's stuff."

"We brung a bunch of clothes," Lilly said. "Some of 'em is in laundry bags. You'll have to wash 'em since I ain't got but a tub and washboard."

"That ain't no problem. I got a washing machine with a wringer. By the way, how are your boys?"

"Fine," Lilly replied. "We still ain't heard from their sister. She took off with that feller and we don't know nothing about where she might be. We ain't seen her in more'n two years."

"I wouldn't worry none, Lilly. I'll bet dollars to doughnuts she's happy as can be."

Lilly took another swig of the whisky. "All your kids is growed up, ain't they?"

"Yeah and they did good for theyselves. My oldest Earl and his wife visited Jeb and me when they was up to Hutchinson last year when he had some free time. It was a short visit but a nice one."

"I reckon it was," Lilly said. She finished her whiskey and stood up. "Well, I do thank you kindly for the likker, Katy. I'll see you later."

"It was nice having you visit, Lilly."

Ten minutes later, the Gilhooly Model A Ford was on the way back to the main road.

CHAPTER 6

The Gilhoolys, flush with the $40 paid them by Shorty Barlow, went to the Safeway Supermarket in Hutchinson to stock up on needed items. Since they had no electricity, they had to settle for canned and packaged food with a long shelf life. During the summer they stored all victuals in a wooden homemade cooler set up in one corner of the kitchen. The front was covered by burlap bags that were kept wet. Meats and other perishables had to be eaten quickly. However, during the freezing winter months, that food could be kept on the back porch without spoiling.

The other purchases in Hutchinson included over-the-counter medicine, first-aid supplies along with small bags of tobacco, cigarette paper and both bath and laundry soap. A few personal hygienic items rounded out their shopping list.

On the way out back to the house, they pulled into the Conoco Filling Station for gasoline and motor oil. This stop also included putting fuel in the five-gallon can kept in the luggage rack. Their final activity before going home, was to head over to the nearby drive-in eatery for hamburgers, French fries, and milkshakes.

All was well with the Gilhoolys.

———

WHEN THE FAMILY ARRIVED AT THE HOUSE, LILLY supervised Horatio in putting away the food in the kitchen cabinets. Since there was no bathroom, acquisitions of toilet paper, medical and health items were put on wall shelves with the groceries. Meanwhile Junior and Cornelius tended to washing the car and doing some minor maintenance under the hood.

After the chores that afternoon, Lilly called them together for another meeting around the kitchen table. "Well, boys, I'm proud of you. We got a good amount of cash money to play with now."

Cornelius spoke up. "Do we have enough to get hooked up to Kansas Gas and Electric?"

"Can't you remember nothing, Corny?" Lilly snapped. "We tried that before and found out we'd have to get the house wired. It would cost way too much money for an electrician to put in wires and plug-ins."

Horatio asked, "What about a telephone, Ma?"

"Well...we really ain't got much use for one right now."

Junior gave his youngest brother a playful punch on the shoulder. "Are you expecting calls from pretty gals?"

"You never know!" Horatio said, winking.

Lilly gave her sons a warm smile. "I'm gonna give you permission to go over to the Acme Trucker Service for a hot meal tonight."

The three young men whooped and clapped.

In truth, they would be doing something more than

just eating at the cafe. While there was good food, the main attraction at the site were the hookers who worked the eighteen-wheelers in the parking lot. Lilly knew her boys were men and had men's physical needs. But neither she nor her sons ever discussed the subject.

"Anything else to tell us, Ma?" Junior asked.

"Nope."

The trio immediately got out the old galvanized bath tub and set it up in the kitchen. They pumped up enough water from the cistern to fill three buckets that would be heated on the woodburning stove.

When the water was at the right temperature for bathing, it was Cornelius' turn to be first, followed by Horatio and Junior. Lilly made them take turns in order to avoid arguments. Junior dipped a pan of hot water from the tub to shave. Cornelius would take care of that after bathing. Horatio had not matured enough to have a beard.

When the grooming was done, the boys dressed, using some of the clothes they had recently stolen. Heavy splashes of Old Spice aftershave on their faces finished up their toilettes.

A wave and bid goodnight was given to Lilly, then the three Gilhooly gallants dashed out the door to the Model A.

———

THE ACME TRUCKERS SERVICE WAS A VERY large and busy enterprise serving commercial truck traffic on U.S. Highway 40. This was one of the main east and west routes established in that part of Kansas. The site excelled with an excellent restaurant, fuel pumps, and a well-equipped repair and maintenance garage. There was also an exchange operated by the Bell Telephone Company. This was used mostly by truckers who needed get in touch with their company headquarters or families.

A large tall neon sign on the site was visible on both directions of the highway.

ACME TRUCKERS SERVICE
FUEL / FOOD / REPAIRS

———

IT WAS DUSK WHEN JUNIOR DROVE ONTO THE service lot. He wheeled past the restaurant, turning toward the truck park where the eighteen-wheelers were situated in a half dozen rows. The drivers had left the motors running, casting a dull pulsating rumbling noise over the scene. This was a meaningful practice since the engines had reached operating temperatures. If they cooled down it would take time to get them restarted.

Junior parked in the usual spot they used when visiting the locale. It was on the back edge of the property line bordered by heavy trees and brush. The brothers got out of the car and Junior turned his attention to Horatio.

"Okay, kid. Get out there and bring back Rhonda."

Horatio didn't need any urging and he rushed off to walk among the trucks to find their favorite whore. He slowed down, looking carefully around the big vehicles for that particular lady of the night. He spotted another roaming hooker looking for customers.

"Have you seen Rhonda around here tonight?"

The woman looked at him and winked. "Whatcha want with her, cutie pie? I got what she's got; only better."

Horatio shook his head. "Your breasts are nowhere near as large as hers."

"Then go find her yourself, squirt," the woman snapped.

Horatio continued down the rows of trucks. He eventually sighted the whore he wanted. She was climbing down from a cab after turning a trick.

"Rhonda!"

The prostitute looked over at the boy and gave him a big smile when she recognized him. "Hey, there, Horatio! Are your brothers with you?"

"You bet! Follow me please. We got the car parked in the usual place."

Rhonda—real name unknown—was a large woman standing close to five feet nine inches. She had a heavy build and muscular legs along with colossal breasts. She didn't wear a brassiere since her customers always wanted to fondle and gaze at those fleshy globes before and during sex with her.

Junior and Cornelius were leaning against the car when Rhonda and Horatio came into view. Rhonda gave them a happy greeting, "Hey now! I been waiting and waiting for you jaspers. Where you been keeping yourselves?"

"Out and about," Junior replied.

"Well, let's get to it," Rhonda suggested. "If you ain't got condoms I can sell 'em for fifty cents each." She looked at Horatio. "Since you got your own special wants, you won't need one."

After the payments for her services, the sexual action was ready to begin. Horatio, who would go last, opened the back door of the Model A for Junior and Rhonda to enter. She always had a jar of petroleum jelly to lubricate the prophylactics of her customers. This was necessary for her personal comfort because of having intercourse more than a dozen times a night.

The old automobile rocked and squeaked as Junior and Cornelius took their turns humping away between Rhonda's strong legs. It had been awhile since the two older Gilhooly boys had been with a woman and it didn't take them long.

After Cornelius left the car, Rhonda sat up on the backseat and Horatio joined her. The youngest Gilhooly enjoyed the hand jobs the woman did with the lubricant. The two would sit side-by-side in the back seat while the boy fondled her breasts as she skillfully stroked him.

Since he was her favorite, she took her time, stopping and starting, until he begged for her to finish.

With that done, Rhonda stepped out of the car and buttoned up. "Are you boys gonna want me again after you eat?"

"You bet!" Junior said. "We'll send Horatio to find you."

"I'll be looking out for him," she said, turning to walk back toward the parked trucks.

The brothers headed for the cafe. The place was crowded with a plethora of truckers and a dearth of tourists. Junior spotted an empty booth and he and his brothers slid into it, settling down to eat.

A gum-chewing waitress walked up to take their orders. "What can I get you boys?"

"We all want the same," Junior said. "Large bowls of chili, soda crackers, slabs of apple pie and coffee."

Service was fast at the truck stop and it was only a few minutes before they were served. The three ate slowly to pass enough time to renew their sexual vigor. When the final cups of coffee were finished, they hurried outside.

Junior sent Horatio out to fetch Rhonda one more time.

———

EARLY THE NEXT SUNDAY MORNING LILLY prepared breakfasts of pancakes and syrup by candlelight. As the boys ate, she gave them their latest marching orders. "Today you'll be going to Harper County. I want you to concentrate on picking up kitchen appliances. Shorty is particularly happy to get 'em and promised me a good price. On the other hand, he told me he don't need shotguns since he's got so many. Rifles and pistols will do. Also don't take no working clothes like bib overalls or Levis. Sears Roebucks and Montgomery Ward can sell 'em cheaper. So get men's suits and fancy stuff like 'at. Especially ladies' dresses. And kids' clothes, too. Ya got it?"

"Yes, ma'am!" they answered in unison.

"And another thing. Be sure and look around them houses for cash money. We can use them greenbacks, too. Ya got it?"

"Yes, ma'am!"

CHAPTER 7

Donna Sue had been mostly by herself in the detective office for the past few weeks. Dwayne had some minor capers that were mostly tailing people for various reasons.

Donna Sue, having finished all her paperwork, filled the empty hours at her desk playing solitaire. One day Maybelle suddenly popped into her mind. She sat back in the chair, thinking about how she and the younger woman had both gone through frustration and humiliation in their lives. Donna Sue gathered up the cards, put them back in the box, then began thinking about how she could help the careworn girl.

LATER THAT SAME AFTERNOON DWAYNE AND Donna Sue left the office and visited a Dillon's Super Market for pick up a few items. With that chore finished they went home to the apartment house. Dwayne stopped to let her out with the grocery bags while he drove over to the parking garage to leave the station wagon. He noticed Donna Sue had been unusually quiet during the drive home. As he walked from the garage to their dwelling he tried to figure out what might be on her mind. He couldn't recall anything he had done that would upset her —at least not lately—and he decided to wait to see how things were going to turn out.

It was Donna Sue's turn to cook supper and she still remained in a mood of puzzling silence as she tended to the task. When they sat down to eat, Donna Sue picked at her salad, then laid her fork down. "Dwayne."

He looked up from his own plate. "What?"

"I've been thinking a lot about Maybelle. She and I have plenty in common."

"Thank God for that," Dwayne stated. "Anyhow, I suppose you're right about that, except you were never a prostitute. Only a welder and a hash slinger."

"I would like to help her out of her unhappy circumstances."

"D'you have anything in mind?"

"I would like to arrange a meeting with her. Maybe a gal's day out. But I'm not sure about contacting her during working hours in the laundry. I've worked in that sort of environment and interrupting a gal during working hours could easily get her in trouble."

"That's the same place my mom worked. They didn't like them girls taking breaks for any reason. I think the best and easiest way of seeing her would be going to her room in the Randall Hotel. You got your keys to the station wagon. Why don't you go over there after supper? It's my turn to do the dishes anyway."

———

DONNA SUE DROVE THE STATION WAGON DOWN East Douglas to her altruistic destination. The neighborhood had two more hostels on the street, but the Randall looked like the best and safest. That didn't surprise her because of the Salvation Army's connection with the hotel. Donna Sue found a parking place a couple of buildings down from the Randall.

The front desk was in an alcove opposite the stairs leading to the upper floors. A middle-age lady was checking out the registration book when Donna Sue came through the front door. She seemed out of place for that particular area of downtown Wichita.

"What can I do for you?"

"I would like to visit Maybelle," Donna Sue explained. "She knows my husband and me. He directed her to the Salvation Army and they rented a room here for her."

"Yes, indeed," the woman said, happy to see that the girl had some outside support. "My name is Daisy Randall. I run the hotel."

Donna Sue liked her right off. "Since the building is in your name, I presume you also own it."

"Oh, yes indeed. It's been in our family for three generations."

"My husband spent some time here when he was a boy," Donna Sue informed her. "He and his mother had been having a hard go of it after his father died and they got some help from the Salvation Army."

Daisy's eyes lit up. "When was that?"

"A long time ago before the war. His name is Dwayne Wheeler."

"Heavens above! I do remember him. He's been mentioned on the radio and in the newspapers for solving some crimes here in Wichita." She suddenly turned serious. "I remember now. His mother died, didn't she? He left after that and joined the Army. I felt so sorry for him. He was devastated."

"He still is," Donna Sue said. "Every once in a while he slips into a period of grief. I suppose he'll always be that way."

"How did you two get to know Maybelle?"

"Dwayne had a temporary job working at the Riverview Hotel as a detective when he met the girl. She was...uh...looking for a room. She didn't have enough money, of course, and he told her about the Salvation Army."

Daisy had a pretty good idea why the penniless Maybelle would go to an expensive hotel, but she kept it to herself. "She came here from the Salvation Army via the Transit Lodging folks. At any rate, the second floor is for the single ladies. You'll find her in room 210."

Donna Sue went up the stairs to the first landing and walked down the hall. She took note of the orderly cleanliness of the place. She knocked on the door when she reached 210.

Maybelle answered the summons and broke into a happy grin. "Missus Wheeler! Come on in. This is a nice surprise."

Donna Sue entered and took a quick look over the small room. It was as spotless as the hallway. A dresser and small chest-of-drawers with a Bible on it were over on the far side. A bed was across the small space with a writing table and chair beside it. A sink with a mirror above it was in front of the bed while a single window looked down on East Douglas.

"Here," Maybelle said. "You sit in the chair. I can park myself on the bed."

Donna Sue noticed there were no cooking facilities in the room. "Where do you eat?"

"Us girls get meal tickets from the Salvation Army for the Tip Top Diner. It's just a block over in the warehouse district."

"That's handy."

"I ain't had to use any of my tickets yet. I'm eating on them fifteen dollars that Mister Wheeler gave me."

Donna Sue decided to cut to the chase. "I came over here, Maybelle, because I want to help you. Now don't get angry with me, but you need new clothes. And I want to help you look a little bit nicer. Just a little bit. I'm talking about makeup."

"I'm a mess, ain't I?"

"I'd be happy if you want me to give you some pointers. We could start by visiting the beauty parlor where I go. It's a high-class place. A good beautician could do a lot for you."

"I guess I could use the rest of the money Mister Wheeler gave me. There's nine dollars left and—"

Donna Sue interrupted. "Dwayne and I are going to pay for everything."

"Oh, no! I couldn't take nothing more from you two, Missus Wheeler!"

"Call me Donna Sue. And Dwayne and I are going to insist that you let us help you." She grinned. "Well, maybe not Dwayne. A mere man couldn't match what you and I can accomplish together. He'd just get in the way of us gals."

Maybelle laughed. "You're prob'ly right."

"After we go to the beauty shop, you and I will do some shopping at Bucks Department Store for some nice clothes."

Maybelle was close to crying. "Why are you doing this for me?"

"I was poor right here in Wichita," Donna Sue said.

"My mom and I took in washing and ironing. We also worked for a company that sent cleaning ladies to office buildings in the evenings. I ended up married to two no good rats. The best job I ever had was at the Boeing Airplane Company during the war. I worked as a welder."

"A welder! That's man's work, ain't it? And you done that?"

"Yes. I did it because there was a shortage of men for the work. This allowed us ladies to do the job. But when the war ended they let all the women go. So from there I went to slinging hash in a diner on West Douglas. That's where I met Dwayne."

"But look at you now!" Maybelle exclaimed.

"I got to this point in my life by myself. I decided I wanted to become a secretary. I took a course that gave me a high school equivalence certificate, then I enrolled in business school."

"I couldn't do that, Donna Sue. I only been to the eighth grade so I never seen the inside of a high school."

"Never put yourself down, Maybelle. At any rate, I got a good job but my boss was taking advantage of me. He got married and wanted me to continue being his mistress." Donna Sue sighed. "But there's more to this. I'll tell you all about it later. It all took place during the time I broke up with Dwayne."

"A man got me to where I am now," Maybelle said. "His name was Billy Joe. He was real nice to me and right handsome, too. So I ran away with him and we went down to Oklahoma City. And...and..."

Donna Sue saw she was about to weep. "Go ahead, honey. I'm listening."

"You'll be ashamed of me, Donna Sue! You will for sure!"

"I guarantee you that I will *not* be ashamed of you, Maybelle."

"We went to a cheap hotel and Billy Joe brought in men and made me have sex with 'em. I didn't want to, but he hit me 'til I did it."

Maybelle broke into deep sobbing and Donna Sue sat down on the bed and put her arms around the girl. "It wasn't your fault, Maybelle. Pretty soon you'll be up in the world and I'm going to help you get there."

Suddenly Donna Sue's emotions swept over her from her own past troubles and Maybelle's present situation. She began weeping softly and pulled a hanky from her purse. The two women sat together in a mutual embrace as both let the tears flow.

CHAPTER 8

The Gilhooly brothers drove from Reno County down through Kingman County and into Harper County. The Sunday morning sun was just edging over the eastern horizon when Junior pulled off and parked on the side of a country road.

Junior stepped out of the car and walked around to the front. Cornelius joined him from the passenger's side. Junior looked around at the open farmland and checked his wrist watch. "We got about an hour before church services. All we gotta do is wait for the sound of bells."

"Then we can hit two or three farmhouses," Cornelius opined. He looked into the car at the backseat. "It looks like Horatio is still snoozing."

Junior laughed. "I bet he's dreaming about Rhoda's tits, huh?"

"I suppose," Cornelius said. He began rolling a cigarette as he sat down on a fender. "Junior, have you ever thought about skedaddling?"

"Yeah. Sister got away. I reckon we could do it, too."

"I'm twenty-two and you're twenty-four," Cornelius

stated. "It seems to me we should hit the road together. I think Horatio would be too young to keep up with us. Besides, Ma would raise holy hell if we took him along."

"You're right about that," Junior stated, pulling out his own bag of tobacco and cigarette papers. "If the two of us do leave, we can rob banks instead of stealing kitchen stuff. We ought to get out of Kansas and go to the west coast or the east coast. I'm thinking on Los Angeles or New York City."

"We could form a gang."

"Them city dudes have a lot of chances to get rich," Junior speculated. "They sell protection to store owners and stuff like 'at." He thought a moment. "Hey! Maybe we could get into gambling like them guys in the movies. That's the way to go."

"What about night clubs?" Cornelius asked. "Remember that movie we saw about rich guys who had a fancy place with dancing girls. Them fellers were gangsters, too. Except they didn't do the crimes. They just planned 'em out and had their mob pull the jobs."

Junior shook his head. "Not a good idea. It'd take too long to set up a nightclub. You gotta have that music stuff, a kitchen to fix fancy food, waiters, cigarette gals and all kinds of shit. I'm telling you the best idea is to get into gambling."

"How would we start?"

Junior sank into a pensive mood for a couple of minutes. "Okay! What we do is check things out first. Right now we don't have no idea where we'd end up in some big city and it wouldn't be very smart to charge in blind, see? Once we know about the things going on and who's doing it, we can pick out a spot to move in and take over."

Cornelius reached into his waist holster and pulled

out the small revolver. "We'll use these to show them city dudes who's the boss, right?"

"Sure. By the time we reach that stage, we'll have a gang. A gang with Tommy guns."

Cornelius put the pistol away just as Horatio stepped out of the back of the Model A. He yawned and greeted his big brothers. "Hey, guys. When do we start?"

The faint sound of a tolling bell could be heard.

"We start right now," Junior announced. "Let's get in the car."

Ten minutes of driving brought the Gilhooly gang to the entrance of a farm house driveway. Junior braked to a stop and studied the layout. "No car nearby. Let's make our move."

He went up the driveway to a place where they could see a backdoor to the house. "Horatio, get outta the car and go up and knock. If anybody answers, just ask him the directions to Harper and we'll go find another place to hit. Got it?"

"Certainly!"

The youngster walked across a patch of grass to the rear entrance. He rapped on the door several times and waited. Then he looked into the kitchen, seeing nobody. The boy grabbed the knob and opened the door. He looked over at Junior and Cornelius and motioned to them that it was okay.

The three walked into the kitchen and were just about to start opening drawers when a boy of about twelve years of age walked in. He was wearing pajamas. "Hi. Are you fellers looking for my Dad?"

Junior quickly recovered. "Ah...buddy...we need to know the way to Harper. Can you help us?"

"Sure. Go on back on the road and turn north to U.S. 160. It'll take you right there."

"Obliged," Junior acknowledged. "Is the rest of your family to church?"

"Yeah. I'm feeling poorly, so they made me stay home."

Cornelius made a move toward his waistband holster, but Junior reached out and stopped him. He turned back to the boy. "You get well quick, okay?"

The kid grinned. "I'll do my best. To tell you the truth I ain't real fond of Sunday school and all that stuff."

"I know what you mean," Junior said. "Thanks for the directions."

He led his brothers out to the car. Junior was furious and turned a quick glare on Cornelius. "Why did you start to go after your pistol?"

"To shoot that guy."

"He was just a kid," Junior pointed out. "He thought we was there to get directions. We got away clean."

Cornelius shrugged. "So what?"

Horatio said, "If you would've killed him we wouldn't have had an opportunity to remain there and steal anything."

Cornelius felt being picked on. "Shut up, you little pecker head."

Junior pulled off to the side of the road and stopped. He hit Cornelius hard in the face with the side of his fist. "If that kid's family found him laying dead and bloody in the kitchen, there would be holy hell to pay. And we damn well would have to hide out for a while. And we'd have to give up what we're doing."

"All right," Cornelius said, reaching for a handkerchief to put on his bleeding nose.

Junior was badly upset. He sat at the wheel, gripping it hard while he took deep breaths. Cornelius tended to his nose and Horatio remained silent in the back seat.

After ten minutes, Junior put the car in gear and got back on the road.

"Keep your eyes open," he mumbled.

———

THE RESIDENCE DID NOT LOOK LIKE IT WAS A farmhouse. It was a large, two-story structure with a short but well-groomed lawn going from the front porch down to the road. Junior stopped at the entrance to the driveway and gave the site a careful study.

Horatio was doing the same. "It looks fine to me, Junior. There isn't an automobile anywhere."

"Let's take a chance," Cornelius suggested. "If anybody's at home we can ask them for directions to Harper."

"Okay," Junior agreed. "There must be a back door. I'll go up and you guys wait in the car." He drove down the driveway to the end where a two-car garage was located. Both doors were open and there was only one auto inside the structure.

Junior got out and went up to the back porch and knocked. He repeated it twice more, than opened the door and stuck his head inside. "Hello! Hello! Is there anybody home?" He waited, then turned to the car and signaled his brothers to join him.

The sight of the kitchen shocked them. It was swanky with a couple of propane stoves and a big table along with two large metal sinks joined together. To the Gilhooly boys it looked like it belonged in a big fancy restaurant. A whole wall of larders and cabinets occupied one wall while numerous pots, pans and skillets were hung up on the hooks of an overhead rack.

Junior's mouth dropped open. "Holy shit! Those are all copper!"

"Is that good?" Horatio asked.

"Damn right!" Junior exclaimed. "You two start hauling them things out to the car while I take a look around the rest of the house."

He went down a hall past a parlor of expensive furniture into another room. It was an office with a heavy desk, bookcases and file cabinets. Junior went to the desk and pulled open a door. A tin box was inside. He pulled it out and opened it. It was filled with twenty dollar bills all in thick packets wrapped with paper strips. He wasn't much on arithmetic, but gave it all a quick excited count. He knew he had ten thousand dollars cash money in his hands.

He shoved the box under his arm and hurried back to the kitchen. Cornelius and Horatio were taking out the last of the pots and pans, and Junior followed them out to the Model A.

"Put that stuff in the luggage rack and get in the car!" Junior ordered.

Cornelius was confused. "What about the rest of the house?"

"Fuck the rest of the house! *Get in the car!*"

His brothers quickly obeyed and Junior drove down to the driveway's entrance. After a quick look both ways to make sure the road was empty, he stepped down on the accelerator and headed north toward Reno County.

Horatio asked, "What's in the box, Junior?"

"Oh, just some odds and ends."

CHAPTER 9

W hitaker's Laundry where Maybelle worked was a thirty-year-old Wichita establishment that operated seven days a week in its original locale in downtown East Douglas.

The employees were all female except for pressers and delivery drivers. The wash-and-dry ladies were expected to work six days a week with one day off. The older female supervisors determined who would get what days. The women who were the best workers had Sundays or Saturdays off. Other less practiced laundresses each had a weekday to rest up, but labored on weekends. Maybelle's breaks came on Wednesdays.

That meant that she and Donna Sue could begin their glamour plan when all the stores were open. The first stop on this sojourn would be the beauty shop that Donna Sue patronized. This was Chez Lydia in the shopping center at Lincoln and Hillside Streets. Donna Sue had made an appointment with Lydia Graham the proprietor, to choose the right hairstyle for Maybelle as well as teach the young girl techniques of makeup. The treatment would also include a manicure.

———

LYDIA GRAHAM WAS A MIDDLE-AGE WOMAN whose talents were evident from her own appearance. She had a svelte body that other women both admired and envied. When walking, her bearing was graceful without effort. All that, along with her stunning hairdos and personal cosmetic applications, produced a self-satisfied lady that gave off an aura of aristocracy and affluence.

Lydia had learned her craft in her sister's beauty shop back in the 1920s. After a couple of years, she left Wichita and went to New York City to pursue her real dream to be an actress. As an intelligent and practical young woman, she had saved enough money for room and board while making the rounds of auditions.

Lydia never achieved that dream of working on the stage, but her early work in the beauty parlor qualified her for jobs doing makeup for performers on Broadway. The girl eventually got a mentor who was a makeup artist in great demand. This was an English woman by the name of Gwendolen Terral. She had worked many years in London's well-known theatrical West End before emigrating to America where she could make more money. Gwendolen ended up being employed by numerous Broadway impresarios for their productions. This English lady and the girl from Wichita worked together throughout many seasons of the New York City stage.

Gwendolen unselfishly passed on her expertise to Lydia. The two became lovers and lived together for eighteen years until the English lady passed away. Lydia was so distraught that she couldn't bear to continue practicing her art in the Broadway theaters. She returned to Wichita in 1940 and founded her own beauty parlor for a quiet existence in the hope of her grief fading away. The shop had an excellent reputation among Wichita women who could afford to patronize it.

Lydia's three women employees in the Wichita parlor had been completely vetted and required to present letters of reference from their last employment. Lydia then put them through a merciless course of instruction capped off by an equally difficult final examination.

As time passed, Lydia fell in love with a client by the name of Doris Lewis. She was the wife of Carl Lewis the owner and operator of the Lewis Construction Company in Wichita.

Doris divorced her husband and moved in with Lydia.

———

DONNA SUE WENT TO THE RANDALL HOTEL ON A Wednesday to go to Chez Lydia for Maybelle's make-over. When Donna Sue drove up to the Randall Hotel to pick her up, the young woman was waiting in front of the building. She hurried across the sidewalk and slid into the passenger's seat. "Hi, Donna Sue!"

Donna Sue laughed out loud. "I'm glad to see you're raring to go."

"I know I ain't gonna be made real perty, but I reckon I can be improved just a little bit."

"I think you can be made beautiful," Donna Sue assured her younger friend. She headed east toward Hillside Street and then turned south. When they reached Lincoln, Donna Sue drove into a small shopping center. Two Cadillacs and a Chrysler Windsor were parked in front of the beauty parlor. They looked out of place at the site where other less sophisticated businesses were established.

The beauty shop had a simple façade. The words CHEZ LYDIA were on the large plate-glass window that had a thick curtain behind it. Most of the female shoppers in the center were housewives who had learned the shop was extremely expensive.

"Here we are!" Donna Sue announced.

Maybelle had a worried expression on her face. "I'm kind of nervous now!"

"C'mon! It's gonna be fun."

The interior of the shop had three partitions for the beauticians to work. Across the narrow floor was a row of hairdryers with customers sitting under them, leafing through the latest ladies and movie magazines.

Lydia Graham was waiting for the arrivals. "Hello, Donna Sue. Come with me." She escorted them to a back room where she worked alone and out of sight. Lydia looked at Maybelle. "So this is our subject, is it?"

Donna Sue introduced the two, and Maybelle's uneasiness had not slackened. "How d'you do, ma'am."

"I am doing fine, thank you, Maybelle. Please take a seat so I can get a good look at you."

"We've already covered shaving legs and arm pits," Donna Sue stated.

"Excellent!"

Maybelle sat facing a mirror as Lydia stood behind her. The first thing she did was run her fingers through the girl's hair. "Ah! We have something wonderful to work with here. Your auburn locks are delightfully full and do you know what they're saying to me, Maybelle?"

"No, ma'am," she replied in confusion.

"They are asking me to arrange your wonderful hair in

way to show off your beauty," Lydia informed her. "But you'll have to help by putting up your hair in curlers every night." She turned to Donna Sue. "I've created a special basket of goodies for Maybelle that will have everything she'll need."

"Did you hear that, Maybelle?"

"Yes," the girl answered, not sure what they were talking about.

"Okay," Lydia said. "Let's go over to a sink and give you a thorough shampoo wash."

Maybelle was set in a chair facing away from a sink. Lydia turned on the faucets and picked up a bottle of shampoo. She gave Maybelle's hair a thorough washing, also massaging her scalp. With that done, the girl was taken back to the mirror.

Lydia combed and snipped, shaping the hair to the length she desired. With that done, she began rolling up the locks in curlers. "Time for the hairdryer," Lydia said. "Then we can turn this cut into a very attractive sight."

She took Maybelle out to the main part of the shop and sat her under one of the hairdryers. She called over to the manicurist. "Tonia, can you spare some time for Maybelle while her hair dries?"

"I sure can," Tonia said. She pushed her manicure cart over to Maybelle and sat down.

Lydia went back to her special room and got the small basket in which she had put shampoo, make-up assortments, curlers, a hand mirror, along with different types of combs and brushes. She showed it to Donna Sue. "Here's what I've picked out for Maybelle. After the girl's hair is dry and her finger nails are taken care of, I'll show her how she'll have to comb and brush those locks every morning. Then we'll take up cosmetics."

Meanwhile out in the shop proper, Tonia took

Maybelle's hands. "Have you ever had a manicure before, Maybelle?"

"I ain't even sure what that is."

"Well, a manicure is a beauty treatment for your fingernails." She put the girl's hands in a bowl of warm water. "This will soften 'em some to make the job easier. Now if we were going to do your toenails, it would be a pedicure. But Lydia wants me to only take care of your fingernails. I see you've been biting them. You better stop that, okay?"

"Okay," Maybelle remarked slightly embarrassed.

"The first thing I'm going to do is use a tool called a pusher to shape around the cuticle. That's the skin at the base of your nails." The manicurist removed Maybelle's hands from the water and went to work. After tending to the thumbs and eight fingers, Tonia began filing and shaping the free edges of the nails. This was followed by a brief buffing. Then a red nail polish was carefully applied.

Maybelle could see that Tonia's work had improved the looks of her hands.

"There's other kinds of manicures and pedicures," Tonia said. "That would be hot oil manicures to clean the cuticles. Maybe later we'll do all that for you." She stood up. "It was nice meeting you, Maybelle."

"I liked getting to know you, too, Tonia."

The manicurist wheeled her table away to another customer just as Lydia appeared to fetch Maybelle. "Follow me and we'll finish your hair."

They returned to Lydia's area where the curlers were removed. Then Maybelle's hair was penned up in a way that would give her a small bouffant on top with wavy traces down to her shoulders. Lydia brushed Maybelle's hair into shape, then stepped back.

"*Voilà!*" the beautician announced.

Maybelle gazed in the mirror at her reflection as Donna Sue joined them. The young girl was amazed at her appearance. "I look kind of perty, don't I?"

Donna Sue patted her on the shoulder. "You look absolutely beautiful, Maybelle."

"Well, now let's talk about make-up," Lydia suggested. She fetched the basket she had prepared. "We'll start with rouge. I've picked a pinkish shade of peach. It will work well on the color of your skin." She took a rouge brush and began to gently apply it to Maybelle's cheeks.

The process continued with Lydia giving instructions, then having Maybelle apply the makeup herself. Eye shadows and mascara were followed by applying lining pencils and lipstick to give more fullness to the girl's lips.

When Maybelle took another close look into the mirror she was amazed. "I *am* perty, ain't I? I never thought I could look like this." The girl started to sob. "I'm...I'm so happy."

"Don't cry!" Lydia warned her. "Your mascara will run!"

Maybelle wisely brought her emotions under control.

Lydia handed her the basket filled with enough proper makeup to last a month. "When one runs out, buy the exact brand and color that I've put in there."

"Yes, ma'am."

Donna Sue was ecstatic. She wrote out a check for thirty dollars. "C'mon, Maybelle! Let's go shopping!"

————

BUCK'S DEPARTMENT STORE, LOCATED AT Broadway and Douglas, was one of Wichita's finest. Donna Sue did all her own shopping there and had a credit card with her signature on it to make purchases.

Maybelle possessed some used practical clothing that she bought at the Salvation Army Store. Later she had received work garments from Whitaker's Laundry that were white and similar to what nurses wore in hospitals. The company management was visited by firms that needed industrial laundering for their employees' uniforms. The sight of women all dressed in clean, white dresses gave a good impression for the laundry.

What Maybelle needed was something a bit more stylish than frumpy second-hand garments. Donna Sue picked out a wool felt roll hat, a poke bonnet, a simple frock, an overcoat for the coming winter, a slack suit, a wool suit, a pair of platform shoes and finally a leather purse with a shoulder strap. The total bill came to $43.50 before sales tax. The time it took to make the purchases and try on all the garments was two hours.

The pair went back to the Randall Hotel and up to the second floor. There was a room in the hall with a washing and rinsing machine, an iron, ironing board and clothes lines. Donna Sue, who had done a lot of work with her mother, took the new clothes and gave them a fresh pressing so Maybelle could wear them as soon as possible.

When the work was done, they went down to Maybelle's room, and the girl announced she had some news for Donna Sue. "I passed my probation period at the laundry and they made me permanent. I got a raise from 50 cents an hour to 70 cents."

"That's wonderful!" Donna Sue exclaimed. "I'm real proud of you, Maybelle."

"And another one of the girls done the same thing, so we're moving in together. Her name is Sally Duncan and she lives here at the hotel, too. We was lucky that a room for two was available. It costs more'n single rooms and has a private bathroom with a tub. But with both of us paying the rent, it's cheaper than the singles."

Donna Sue announced, "We must celebrate. Dwayne and I will take you and Sally out to dinner. You can wear your frock."

"Well," Maybelle said, "maybe it'd be better if I dressed in one of my other dresses. Sally ain't got nothing like that frock."

"Of course, Maybelle," Donna Sue said, pleased that the girl had a considerate side. "Dwayne and I will be very happy to meet your friend."

CHAPTER 10

Junior Gilhooly waited until he could be alone with Cornelius in his room before revealing the ten thousand dollars. "Sit down."

Cornelius sat on the bed, slightly confused. "What's going on?"

Junior reached up and grabbed the tin box he had hidden on a rafter. "This is what I found in that last house. It's got ten thousand dollars in it."

"I thought you said there was just odds and ends in the box. And how do you know there's ten thousand dollars in it?"

"Let me explain something to you. I looked inside the fucking box and saw fucking packets of twenty dollar bills. There was fifty twenty dollar bills in each of ten packets. That means each packet had a thousand dollars! There's ten thousand dollars here."

"Okay. You was always sorta good at arithmetic, Junior."

"Remember how fancy that house was?" Junior asked. "Well, that means the farmer living there is really rich. He prob'ly gathered up ten thousand bucks in cash money for some reason. Maybe farm equipment or building a new barn or buying some land or something."

"How come you waited to tell me?"

"If I'd've said anything before we got home, Horatio would have heard me."

"You don't want him to know, right?"

"O'course not! He'd tell Ma. And we want to get the hell away from them two."

"Oh, yeah! And be gangsters in big cities," Cornelius said.

Junior gave him a warning glare. "And I don't want you to get into this box, understand? If you do, I'll whip your ass like you was a stepchild."

Cornelius, who had been pounded by Junior's fists in the past, spoke up fast. "I ain't a stepchild!"

"You idjit! I said I'd beat you up like you *was* one."

"Oh. Anyhow, I swear I won't get into the box, Junior."

"Good. Now listen up. Here's how we're gonna work this thing. We can't just go off and leave Ma and Horatio in the lurch. So we'll keep up with these Sunday burglaries 'til they got enough money to get by for a while. That's when we'll head for some big city and open up a gambling joint."

"What about the car?" Cornelius asked. "Ma and Horatio won't be able to go nowhere without the car."

"Jesus Christ! What the hell do you think we're gonna do, drive an old Model A Ford into Chicago or New York? We'll buy another really nice car for us."

"What kind?"

"Just a nice car," Junior said. "Maybe we'll get a Cadillac. How's that?"

"That's fine."

"And after our casino—"

Cornelius interrupted him. "What's a casino?"

"A goddamn *casino* is a goddamn *gambling joint!*"

"Oh."

Junior continued. "After our casino is making lots o' money, we'll start sending some to Ma and Horatio. Eventually we'll have 'em come out and live with us in our mansion. Do you understand ever'thing I been saying?"

"Yes."

"I ain't made up my mind whether we go west to Los Angeles or east to New York."

"I got an idea!" Cornelius exclaimed. "Let's go west to Hollywood so's we can have pretty movie stars for girlfriends."

Junior was thoughtful for a moment. "Well...well...let me think on that."

"I want Lana Turner."

"Let's concentrate on more important things right now."

"All right," Cornelius conceded, "but I got dibs on Lana Turner."

"Okay. Or we could go east to Chicago or New York City."

"I want to go to Hollywood!" Cornelius insisted.

"Let me set something straight for you, butthead. Ever'thing is gonna be what *I* want. So don't start making dibs on anything. Remember how I kept you out of trouble when we was in the can in Lansing?"

"Yeah."

"I'm the smart brother, see?" You're the dumbass, see?"

"Horatio is a lot smarter'n you."

"Well I'm smart enough to keep you outta trouble

when we make our moves to form a gang and run a casino."

"Okay, Junior."

Junior put the box back on the rafter. "So let's just carry on like we usually do to get some money for Ma and Horatio while I figger out a plan."

"Okay."

"Now let's go downstairs and see what Ma has fixed for supper."

———

DWAYNE HELD THE DOOR OF THE CONTINENTAL Grill open for Donna Sue, Maybelle and Sally Duncan. Maybelle's friend was plain and chubby with a freckled face and red hair. She had lived in Wichita all her life, but had never been in any of the city's restaurants. The closest she had gotten to eating out was going to the window of a Kings-X takeout kiosk for one of their hamburgers-in-a-box.

Donna Sue led the way to an empty booth. Dwayne and Donna Sue scooted in on one side while the two girls occupied the other. A waitress immediately appeared, giving a cheerful greeting while passing out menus.

"Can I get you folks something to drink while you're making up your minds?"

"An ice tea for me," Donna Sue said. Dwayne asked for an Orange Crush while Maybelle ordered a Coke. Sally hesitated, then ordered a Coke like Maybelle.

"I'll be right back," the waitress promised, going to fetch the drinks.

Dwayne took a look at Sally and immediately sensed she was ill at ease. He knew how she must feel, being with

Donna Sue and Maybelle. He cleared his throat and said, "I think I'm gonna get a grilled cheese sandwich with French fries when the waitress comes back."

"I want French fries but with a hamburger," Maybelle stated.

"Me, too," Sally said.

"Hey, y'know what?" Dwayne remarked, "I believe I'll take a hamburger like you girls instead of a grilled cheese sandwich. That sounds a lot better to me."

Donna Sue was surprised by his changing his mind, then realized he was showing consideration for Sally's feelings. This was one of those times when she was suddenly struck with extra love for him.

"I want a hamburger and fries, too," Donna Sue said. "That sounds like a really nice lunch."

When the waitress came back with the drinks, Dwayne quickly spoke up. "We all want the same thing. Hamburgers and French fries. Make 'em medium well."

"You got it folks!" the waitress said cheerfully.

As they waited for the food, Dwayne remarked, "Donna Sue told me you two were roommates."

"Yes," Maybelle said. "We got a room on the third floor with two twin beds and a private bathroom. We like it a lot."

Sally said, "Maybelle and me both work at Whitaker's Laundry."

"That's interesting," Dwayne said. "Y'know, my mom worked in that same laundry a long time ago. We lived in the Randall Hotel, too. That was after my dad died and we didn't have any place else to go. The Salvation Army helped us a lot. I'll always be grateful for how nice they was to us. Then my mom died and I joined the Army."

Sally looked at Dwayne, now at ease and feeling a rapport with him. "Life can be hard at times, can't it?"

The waitress showed up with their orders, laughing. "I guess I can just put these down anywhere since they're all the same."

Dwayne caught Sally's eye. "Yes. We're all the same."

Sally smiled at him, and said, "I'm sure hungry!"

CHAPTER 11

The next burglary mission for the Gilhooly brothers was Sumner County, an area that ran south from Sedgwick County down to the Oklahoma state line. Junior wanted to avoid going through Harper County where they had already pulled a couple of jobs. For that reason, he chose a roundabout way to their destination. It was midnight when the boys left home in their trustworthy Model A Ford. The route they took was south on State Highway 17 down to U.S. 54 in Wichita.

When they traveled through the city, Cornelius viewed the metropolitan area with excitement. "Hey, Junior. Is Wichita bigger'n Los Angeles or New York City?"

"They're all about the same size."

Horatio spoke up. "For heaven's sake! You could put ten or twelve Wichitas in those metropolises. Why do you ask that, Corny?"

Cornelius glared at him. "None of your damn business!"

"I was just asking!"

The trip continued on U.S. 54 to Augusta, then Junior headed south on U.S. 77 all the way to Winfield. From there he drove on country roads that led into Sumner County. The trip ended at 7 a.m. when Junior pulled over and stopped. He killed the engine and yawned. "You two stay awake and listen for church bells. After all that driving I need some shuteye."

———

CORNELIUS SHOOK JUNIOR AWAKE AT AN HOUR past dawn. "There ain't no church bells, but I just seen a car yonder at the crossroads. The people in it was dressed in their Sunday-Go-To-Meeting clothes."

Junior sat up and stretched. "What direction was they going?"

"Right to left."

"Then we'll just go up to that crossroad and I'll turn left to right."

Horatio spoke up. "You'll be going east. I know that because that's where the sun comes up. It always shows up in the east. If we were up the road facing the other way, you'd turn—"

"Shut up!" Junior snapped.

They traveled on the road to a spot where a barbed wire fence began. A quarter of mile beyond that was an opening in the enclosure. A farmhouse was visible just beyond that location. Junior drove up the empty driveway to the house and stopped.

"Let's go, boys!"

Cornelius and Horatio followed their big brother up to the porch. He turned the doorknob and stepped inside. "Horatio, get those two kitchen appliances over by the sink and take 'em out to the car. Corny, come with me to check out the rest of the house."

All three froze in place at the sudden appearance of an old man carrying a cane.

"Who're you?" the oldster called out.

Junior immediately noticed that the cane was white and red. The old man's eyes were also clouded over as if by heavy cellophane, and Junior realized he was blind.

"I asked who you are," the old-timer repeated.

Junior turned and motioned for Horatio to go out to the car with the food chopper and coffeemaker. He turned his eyes back to the blind man. "We're looking for directions to Wellington." He forced a laugh. "I reckon we got confused somewhere."

The blind man wasn't buying the statement. "Get out of here right now! You ain't got no business in this house."

Cornelius moved over to the kitchen wall, but the old man sensed his location and swung his cane, striking the intruder on the shoulder. Junior quickly stepped forward and drove a fist into the oldster's face. The man stumbled backward and went down, striking his head on the floor. He twitched a few times, then ceased moving.

"Shit!" Junior exclaimed. He grabbed Cornelius' arm and pulled him toward the door.

———

DWAYNE AND DONNA SUE BEGAN THEIR MONDAY workweek in the usual manner. She called the Reliable Answering Service to see if there were any messages. The operator Millie had one for Dwayne. Donna Sue wrote it down and hung up.

"You have a phone call, Dwayne."

He left his desk and walked around the partition. He didn't recognize the number. Dwayne picked up the handset and dialed. A phone rang and a brisk male voice announced, "K.B.I. office."

The fact he'd been contacted by the Kansas Bureau of Investigation surprised him. "This is Dwayne Wheeler returning a call to this number."

"Ah, good! Hello, Dwayne, this is Harry Philbin. We need to see you."

"Oh," Dwayne said, remembering the K.B.I. officer who had a small part in the Wichita Undercover Caper. "What can I do for you, Harry?"

"I got a case for you. Are you gonna be available this morning?"

"Sure. Do you want to meet some place?"

"No. I'll come up to your office."

Dwayne hung up and turned to Donna Sue. "It seems Harry Philbin of the K.B.I. has a caper for me. Whoops! I mean a *case*. They're more sophisticated than me."

"More sophisticated than *I*," his wife corrected him.

Dwayne felt like making a joke. "More sophisticated than you, too?"

"T'aint funny, McGee," she replied, reciting a standing line from the popular *Fibber McGee and Molly* radio program.

They only had to wait ten minutes before Harry Philbin stepped through the door carrying a brief case. The K.B.I. agent wasted no time. "We can use your services, Dwayne. There's been a series of burglaries of farm houses." He looked at Donna Sue. "You must be his wife."

"His wife and secretary," she said. "I'm Donna Sue."

"Let's go into my office," Dwayne suggested. "Should Donna Sue take notes?"

"It wouldn't hurt," Philbin replied.

The three went around the partition and sat down. Philbin began with, "The K.B.I. is up to its ears in narcotics cases. They've really been growing in numbers since the end of the war. We were going to call in the Highway Patrol to take care of the burglaries but they're shorthanded as it is."

Dwayne grinned. "So I'm second choice, hey?"

"Don't put yourself down," Philbin said. "We remembered you from that case on those eastern gangsters coming into Kansas. You did a hell of a good job." He reached into his briefcase and pulled out a packet of papers. "Here's the information. Take a look at it."

Dwayne took the documents and began reading aloud. "Burglaries on farms...these break-ins are done on Sunday mornings...all of 'em! I wonder what makes Sunday mornings so special."

"That's when the farmers and their families go to church."

"So?"

Philbin grinned. "You don't know much about Kansas farmers, do you?"

"I know they plant and harvest wheat and have done a lot voting in the past to keep me from enjoying my liquor or betting on horse races."

"You didn't know they rarely lock their doors. And that includes when they go to church."

"Oh, yeah. My good friend Tommy Brady lives on a farm outside of Augusta. He never locks up when he leaves his house." He turned his attention back to the report. "It seems the break-ins have occurred in Kingman, Harper and Sumner Counties. Wait! There is a report about an assault on a blind guy. How do you know this particular one was done by the burglars?"

"Two kitchen appliances were missing from the house," Philbin informed the shamus. "So! What do you say? D'you want the assignment?"

"Sure do," Dwayne said, laying the report down.

"Good. You're gonna be sworn in as a temporary agent of the K.B.I. However, the badge and I.D. card will be no different than permanent members of the bureau carry. And you have all the authority as we do. Understand?"

"Sure, but I'm a little surprised. Who's gonna swear me in?"

"Me," Philbin said. "I've got a badge and an I.D. card for you." He looked over at Donna Sue. "You can sign as a witness." He swung his eyes back to Dwayne. "Now raise your right hand and repeat after me. I—say your name—do hereby swear..."

Within thirty seconds Dwayne Wheeler private investigator became Dwayne Wheeler K.B.I. agent.

CHAPTER 12

Lilly Gilhooly sat at the kitchen table with her three sons. Each had a cup of freshly brewed coffee sitting in front of him. The mood was somber after Junior related the incident with the old blind man.

"I know I should've checked him before we left, Ma. But ever'thing happened so damn fast the only thing I could think of was to get the hell outta there. So I don't know if he's dead or not."

"Well, you can't be blamed for that," Lilly allowed. "But if he's dead, we could be facing murder charges at worse or manslaughter at best." She took a couple of sips of coffee. "Maybe they'll think he fell down. Old folks is always falling down. And he was blind."

Junior shook his head. "We took a food chopper and a coffeemaker out to the car. I didn't think to take 'em back. So they'll know somebody was in there stealing stuff when he tumbled down."

"With a bit of luck," Lilly said, "things should turn out good enough. Are you certain nobody seen you drive away?"

"I'm sure of that," Junior said. "We didn't see nobody 'til we was well on the road to Winfield."

"We can't let up now," Lilly said. "We really need to raise some cash money. Next Sunday I want you to go to Marion County."

"Sure, Ma."

"Just be careful."

The session was over, and Lilly went to her bedroom for a nap. Horatio was sent out to wash the car and the two older brothers went upstairs to Junior's bedroom. Cornelius walked over to the window and looked out over the flat prairie countryside.

Junior sat on the bed and rolled a cigarette. "I'm perty sure things is gonna turn out good."

"Me, too," Cornelius said.

"But if we get an inkling things is fucked up, you and me gotta get the hell outta here if we want to go to a big city. I ain't in no mood to be sent back to Lansing, 'specially if we would get hung."

Cornelius turned from the window. "I think we got to really give them plans of ours some serious thought now."

"I've been thinking on that, too," Junior said. "We gotta get us a car, Corny."

"That ain't no problem. We sure as hell got enough money."

"The Ace Used Car lot in Hutchinson has some good cars. And Clayton Timmons runs things honest in his business."

"Yeah," Cornelius agreed. "But what's Ma gonna say when we show up with a car?"

"If we buy one from Timmons, that won't be a problem. He's got that garage behind his office where his mechanics do repairs. There's also a big space in the back where he stores cars for folks who are gonna be out of town for a spell."

"I get it, big brother. We buy a car then leave it there 'til we need it."

"Meanwhile, Ma wants us to head out to Marion County," Junior reminded him. "It'll be another round-about trip since we got to go north to Harvey to McPherson to drive into Marion."

"Okay," Cornelius said. He paused a minute. "Before we go, why don't we take a trip to see Rhonda at the truck stop?"

"Didn't you hear Ma? She's says things is tight right now."

Cornelius argued, "But we got enough of our own money to do it."

"Goddamn it, Corny! We don't want Ma or Horatio to know we got that cash!"

"Oh yeah. I forgot."

———

DWAYNE WHEELER'S FIRST ERRAND IN THE K.B.I. case was to make a call on the Sedgwick County Sheriff's Department to see his friend Lieutenant Dave Mason at the south substation in Planeview. That community, filled with blue-gray frame housing, had been rented to aircraft workers during World War II. Some Boeing employees still lived there because of the cheap rent, while a large influx of African-Americans had become recent residents for the same reason.

Dwayne drove into the Planeview shopping center where the local community had offices, a movie theater, grocery store, a couple of other businesses and the sheriff's substation. The shamus had been furnished a 1940

Chevrolet Coupé by the K.B.I. for the investigation. That had been a pleasant surprise for him. He always hated to use his precious Nash Suburban on capers.

Dwayne pulled up in front of the building where a pair of patrol cars were parked. When he walked into the substation he nodded to the deputy at the reception post and continued to the back of the room where Lieutenant Mason kept his desk. Mason looked up from reading the latest interoffice dispatches.

"Hello, Dwayne. What brings you down here?"

"Hi, Dave," Dwayne said. "Have you got any burglary reports in those documents you're reading?"

"O'course. Why do you ask?"

Dwayne reached into his inside jacket pocket and pulled out the K.B.I. badge. "I have a new employer."

"Christ, Dwayne! Where'd you steal that?"

Dwayne next pulled out his wallet and showed the official I.D. card. "I've been sworn in, see? I'm a working Bureau agent. There have been some burglaries on farms in various counties and I've been charged with doing the investigation. The K.B.I. is understaffed and busy with the sudden narcotics activity. They want to nip it in the bud, so to speak."

"They got the best guy to help out," Mason said. "You've done some damn fine work for the Feds. So what's this about burglaries?"

"It seems there's a gang that's going through King-man, Harper and Sumner counties, breaking into farmers' homes. They do it on Sundays because that's when the wheat growers are in church—"

Mason broke in. "—they don't lock their doors, right?"

"Bingo!"

"Well, it's not happened here in rural Sedgwick

County. All our breaking-and-entering crimes are in Wichita proper."

"Okay," Dwayne said. "I wanted to find out if I could get a good start in the Sedgwick sheriff's reports."

"If any such crimes are committed on local farms, I'll let you know."

"That'd be big help, Dave."

"Congratulations on your new position in fighting crime."

"I appreciate the encouragement," Dwayne said.

He left the substation and went back to the Chevy Coupé. It was time to launch the caper.

CHAPTER 13

D wayne drove across the Kingman County line a half hour after leaving Planeview. The first thing he did was follow proper law enforcement protocol by checking in the with local sheriff at the county seat. He showed his credentials and informed the man he would be in his jurisdiction working on the burglaries. After a few questions, the shamus *cum* K.B.I. agent learned there had been no more break-ins.

With those formalities taken care of, Dwayne went back to the Chevy and pulled out the case information files he kept under the front seat. He studied the three maps of the counties where the crimes were committed. The Kingman chart indicated his first call would be the Jackson farm.

Dwayne drove out of town to the site of the robbery. After parking, he went to the front porch and knocked on the door.

A rather plain lady, appearing to be in her late thirties or early forties, appeared. She was dressed in Sears

Roebuck or Montgomery Ward style and wore glasses. "Hello."

"Hello," Dwayne said "I reckon you're Missus Jackson."

"I am."

"I'm Agent Wheeler of the Kansas Bureau of Investigation," he stated, displaying his badge. "I'm here to ask you folks a few questions about the robbery that happened here awhile back."

"Please come in," Mrs. Jackson said, opening the door. She called out, "Carl! There's a lawman here to talk to you. He's from the state something-or-other."

Her husband appeared from the back of the house as Dwayne stepped inside. The farmer was puzzled. "We already told ever'thing to the sheriff."

"I know that, Mister Jackson. But it's turned out the robbers that broke in here have been pulling jobs in this county along with Harper and Sumner."

Jackson frowned. "I know who did it. Some of them criminals that live in Wichita did it. That place is crawling with bad people."

"What got stolen from you, Mister Jackson?"

Mrs. Jackson spoke up. "They took a skillet, a Mixmaster, a coffeemaker and some money I had in an empty coffee can. I don't know the exact amount, but I'd guess at around ten or fifteen dollars."

Now Jackson cut in. "They stole my Winchester carbine and Remington shotgun, too. Prob'ly wanted to use 'em to rob one of them likker stores in Wichita and get drunk."

Mrs. Jackson nodded her agreement. "There's nothing but cigarette smokers and beer guzzlers living in that den of evil."

Dwayne was anxious to get to the chase. "How did they get into your house?"

"They just walked in big as you please," Jackson grumbled.

"Was your doors locked?"

"No! Us farmers don't normally need to do that. Out here we don't have robbers hanging around like in Wichita."

"So it wasn't breaking-and-entering then," Dwayne said.

Jackson shook his head. "I guess not."

"Well, thanks for the information," Dwayne said. "The K.B.I. is gonna investigate this thoroughly. In the meantime, if anything else happens, inform your county sheriff. He'll get in touch with us. I've already arranged for that. We'll take the perpetrators into custody and get back as much of your stolen items as possible."

"Just go on down to Wichita and dig around," Jackson said. "That's where you're gonna find 'em."

Dwayne's next visit was to the second house that had been robbed. The crime committed there was similar to the Jacksons. Kitchen appliances, some clothing and yet another coffee can with loose bills and change in it. Maybe Farmer Jackson was right about Wichita bad guys being involved. Dwayne considered calling on the Wichita fence Pete Driscoll. It might be a good idea to check in with him.

———

IT WAS LATE AFTERNOON WHEN DWAYNE MADE his next call in Harper County. After checking in with the local law, he went out to the Shaw farm. He was impressed by the elegance of the house and buildings. This was obviously the home of a farmer who had gotten rich raising wheat.

Tom Shaw invited Dwayne into the house, then called his wife Emily and daughter Fiona. Everyone sat down in the living room. The inside of the house was as elegant as the outside.

"I sure hope you can get my money back," Shaw said.

"We'll sure try," Dwayne promised, scanning the report. "It says here they took thirty thousand dollars from a desk drawer."

"Yeah. It was for buying a new combine and some other implements to modernize my operation," Tom said. "I had it insured. The bank insisted on it before giving me the loan. I don't reckon I'll ever get it back, huh?"

"You never know," Dwayne said. "What else was taken?"

Mrs. Shaw spoke up. "They took all my copper kitchenware."

Fiona the daughter added, "It's real expensive and excellent to cook in."

Dwayne made a note of the loss. "Was that insured?"

"No," Tom stated. "We don't have any crime out here, so I never thought of that."

Dwayne's detective instincts kicked in as he made a note. He looked up at Shaw. "So you had *all* that money in a desk drawer?"

"Uh...yeah...sure. That's the way we do our business... with cash money." He cleared his throat. "Yeah. Cash money. That's the game out here."

"It's kind of risky, isn't it?" Dwayne asked, thinking that there could have been more money kept somewhere else. If the farmer got an insurance payment on the whole amount he would score a hefty profit.

Shaw said, "It's risky to have cash money in the house

if Wichita criminals are going to start coming up here to loot the farms."

The daughter showed a frown. "I just hate knowing that some bad people from Wichita were in our house."

Dwayne was slightly irritated. "There's some real decent people in Wichita."

"I got a subscription to the *Wichita Eagle Sunday Paper*," Shaw remarked. "And it's filled with stories about robberies and even cold-blooded murder in every issue."

Dwayne stood up, knowing better than to get into an argument. "Well, thank you, Mister and Missus Shaw. We'll be in touch if we get any information."

Dwayne went out to the car and checked the map before driving off. His next visit would be to the Buford family.

———

THE BUFORD FARM HAD NOT BEEN ROBBED, BUT three suspicious men had shown up while Danny Buford had been home from church because of a bad cold. Dwayne saw Harold Buford and Danny working on a tractor as he drove up their driveway. They gave him friendly waves as most farmers do even to strangers. "Howdy. What can we do for you?"

Dwayne went through the routine of identifying himself and showing his badge. "I'd like to talk to your son about the three guys that visited your farm while he was home alone."

"Sure," Buford said.

Dwayne pulled out a mug shot album he was carrying. It had photos of known burglars in Wichita. Buford and his son led the way into the house.

Mrs. Loretta Buford was shelling peas and looked up at their entrance. "Who's our visitor, Harold?"

"He's a lawman. He wants Danny to look at some pictures."

Loretta left her peas to follow the men into the parlor. As soon as everyone sat down, the father nodded toward his son. "Tell the officer what happened."

"Well," Danny began, "I didn't go to church that Sunday 'cause I had a bad cold. I was up in my room when I heard the screen door open and close. I thought maybe mom and dad had come home early, so I went downstairs."

Dwayne asked, "Were they making loud noises?"

"Not really. When I walked into the kitchen, the three of 'em looked up kind of surprised. So I asked 'em if they were looking for my dad. They said no, that they were lost and needed directions to Harper. I told 'em and they left."

"What did they look like, Danny?" Dwayne inquired.

"Two of 'em were husky guys. It looked like they would be good football players. There was a third one who was smaller and kind of sissy looking."

Dwayne quickly scribbled the information down. "Did they call each other by name?"

"I only heard one and that was 'Junior'," Danny replied. "He was the biggest and seemed like the boss."

"Now that's the best information I've gotten so far," Dwayne said.

Harold smiled and patted his son's shoulder. "Way to go, boy!"

Dwayne handed the album to Danny. "This is a rogue's gallery. It's filled with mug shots of known burglars in the Wichita area. I would appreciate you looking through it to see if you recognize any 'em."

"Shouldn't they be in jail?" Mr. Buford asked.

"Some of 'em prob'ly are," Dwayne answered. "Others have served their sentences or are on parole or probation."

Danny opened the album and began paging through it as his parents joined him. Dwayne was glad to see that Danny was taking his time. Dwayne sat back, wishing he could smoke a cigarette but there were no ashtrays in view.

Mrs. Buford looked at one picture and exclaimed. "That feller looks real mean."

"He prob'ly is," her husband said.

A few pages later, Mrs. Buford gasped. "Look at that one on the bottom of the page. Why he's just a baby!"

"He's not a baby," Mr. Buford said. "He's a criminal. He prob'ly don't look his age."

Thirty minutes later Danny closed the album. "I didn't see anybody that looked like the three that was here. A couple were close, but I couldn't be sure of 'em."

Dwayne got up and took the album. He shook hands and thanked parents and son before departing for Sumner County.

———

THE SUN WAS STILL UP WHEN DWAYNE ARRIVED in Sumner County. The sheriff wasn't present in the jail, but a deputy was on duty. After Dwayne showed his K.B.I. identification, the local lawman gave him a one-sentence description of the foiled burglary.

"They was chased away by Morgan Clover, an old blind guy."

Dwayne was surprised. "How far did he go after 'em?"

"Not far at all. They hauled off and punched him."

The shamus wasn't interested in second-hand information. "Okay. It's getting late so I better get out to their farm before suppertime."

When he arrived at the Clover house, he could see four people sitting on the front porch. As soon as he got out of the car, they gave him the friendly farmer wave. He waved back and walked up to the porch. "I'm from the Kansas Bureau of Investigation," he announced with a friendly smile as he showed his badge. "I'm here to look into the assault on a Mister Morgan Clover."

The old man sitting on the porch swing raised a white and red cane. "That's me."

A younger man was seated on a chaise lounge. He stood up and offered his hand. "I'm Mathew Clover, his son. The lady sitting on the swing here is my wife Esther. You're welcome to have a seat, if you'd care to."

"I won't be staying that long," Dwayne said. "Thanks anyway." He turned his attention to Morgan. "Can you give me a rundown on what happened to you?"

"Well, sure. Mathew and Esther was at church, but I don't like going."

Mathew interjected, "He don't like going because he knows ever'body is looking at him."

"I ain't completely blind," Morgan said. "I see shadowy stuff. But I know they're staring at me. I prefer to stay home and listen to the preacher on the radio."

Mrs. Clover joined in. "There's a broadcast of Reverend Folgers from our church ever' Sunday."

"So you see I'm really at worship in my room by the radio," Morgan stated.

Dwayne was getting impatient. "Can you tell me about the attack on you?"

"Well, I was in my bedroom and heard some scuffling and talking down in the kitchen. I couldn't imagine who it was, but as I went down the stairs I could hear men's voices and they was up to no good. I got mad at 'em and they kinda spread out and I swung my cane and hit the one to my left. And that's all I remember."

"I guess you don't know how many there was," Dwayne said.

"Hell, yes! There was three of 'em. That's how many shadowy shapes I saw."

Mrs. Clover spoke up once more. "They took my chopper and coffeemaker. We figger they're from Wichita. Nobody else would do such a thing around here."

Dwayne had grown weary of hearing his hometown put down. "I wouldn't jump to conclusions, folks."

"There's Democrats down there," Mathew said.

"That don't mean nothing," Morgan countered. "F.D.R. was a Democrat and a fine man. He helped us farmers a lot."

"He's dead and them Democrats are running wild!" Mrs. Clover snapped. "It's the Republicans that's gonna help us from now on."

Dwayne tipped his hat and left the porch, walking over to his car.

CHAPTER 14

Dwayne got back to Wichita at eleven p.m. Since he was driving the K.B.I. coupé, he parked it at the curb in front of the apartment house.

Donna Sue was sitting up in bed waiting for him as she read a short story in *The Ladies Home Journal*. When she heard Dwayne's key in the lock, she got up and went out to the living room in time to see him walking into the apartment. She gave him a quick kiss and hug.

"How'd it go?"

"I learned we're living in a hell hole filled with demons and devils."

"What in the world are you talking about?" Donna Sue asked, taken aback.

"And Democrats. We're living in a hell hole filled with demons, devils *and* Democrats. Here in Wichita, that is. One lady said ever'body that lives here is a cigarette smoker and a beer guzzler."

"I know what you need, my gallant husband. A glass of Jack Daniels Sour Mash Whisky."

Dwayne put his administrative material on an end

table and hung up his hat and coat on the hat rack by the door. He sat down on the couch, anticipating his favorite liquor. Donna Sue handed him the glass of whiskey and he took a big swallow. He pulled a pack of Lucky Strikes from his shirt pocket, and lit one. "I may be a cigarette smoker but I guzzle whiskey not beer."

Donna Sue went to the kitchen and came back with a glass of Chardonnay and sat down. "See? We have wine guzzlers in Wichita, too."

"Wichita looked real good to me when I crossed the city limits."

"How many break ins and enters are you investigating?"

"None," Dwayne said.

"How can that be?"

"The farmers evidently do not lock their doors," Dwayne explained.

"Let me get this straight. They *don't* lock their doors?"

"You've won the sixty-four-dollar question, my dear. So the burglars did not have to do any breaking and entering. They just sashayed in and sashayed back out with their loot."

"I'm still confused."

"When the farmers go to church on Sunday mornings they leave their doors unlocked," Dwayne explained. "In fact every time they leave the house they don't bother to lock their doors."

Donna Sue was thoughtful for a moment, then suddenly stated, "That means Wichita smokers and guzzlers aren't involved. It's as simple as that."

Dwayne knew this was going to be one of the times when Donna Sue would display the power of her intellect.

He took a small sip of whiskey, then begged, "Explain yourself, woman!"

"It's really very simple. The criminals knew ahead of time that nobody would be home on Sunday mornings. And they're aware the doors aren't locked. But we smokers and guzzlers have no knowledge of unlocked doors. We would just smash their doors in."

Dwayne held his glass halfway up to his mouth at the revelation. "By God! You're right."

"Damn right I'm right!"

Dwayne suddenly laughed. "You know something? I'm gonna solve this caper and make them eat crow about good ol' Wichita. And there's another thing."

"Do tell me what it is, darling," Donna Sue said.

"There's one farmer—a wealthy one—who claimed the burglars took thirty thousand dollars from a desk drawer in his house. He explained he was going to purchase a new combine and other farm machinery with the cash. The way he said it made me suspicious. I'll bet a dollar to a doughnut that he had part of that money in another place. He mentioned the insurance he had taken out for it. So! When the insurance company pays—"

Donna Sue interrupted. "—they'll be paying him more cash money that he lost. And another thing. What were the burglars stealing from those farmers?"

"Mostly kitchen appliances."

"Kitchen appliances, huh?" Donna Sue remarked. "Then there's a fence out there in the hinterlands that is buying things that would be in big demand. He could resell them cheaper than what is charged in legitimate stores."

"If that's the case," Dwayne said, "there could be merchants buying that stuff. That would be store owners who aren't the curious types when it comes to getting merchandise to sell."

"That makes sense," Donna Sue agreed. "And if their prices are lower than the catalogs, then the locals would go to their stores to purchase cheaper goods."

"Here's another thought. Maybe the salesman is passing himself as working for churches or other charitable organizations."

Donna Sue finished her wine. "All those probabilities and possibilities are gonna make your job that much more difficult."

"Sweetie, can I have another whiskey please?"

———

JUNIOR GILHOOLY HAD HIS BROTHER CORNELIUS with him as he drove into Hutchinson. Their destination was the Timmons Used Car lot located on the western edge of the community. The distinctive sound of their Model A Ford engine driving up caught Clayton Timmons' attention sitting in his office. He went to the window, catching sight of the brothers coming to a halt. He walked out of the small building and approached the old automobile, walking slowly around it. "Somebody has been taking damn good care of this old beauty."

Junior stepped out. "This ain't for trading in. We're looking for an automobile to buy. And we got cash money."

These two potential customers didn't strike Timmons as the sort who would have a lot of greenbacks. "Mmm," he mused. "Just how much do you fellers want to spend?"

"We got around two hunnerd dollars."

"Cash?" Timmons inquired.

"Yeah," Junior answered. "And we'd like to store the car we buy in your garage."

"For how long?"

"Not more'n a couple or three months," Junior told him. "How much would that be?"

"At five dollars a month, not more'n fifteen bucks."

"That's fine," Junior assured him.

Timmons displayed a wide grin. "C'mon with me. I got a real clean '41 Oldsmobile that was brought in by a little ol' lady from Arlington. The mileage on it is incredibly low. Seventy-five bucks. I think you'll like it."

He and the two Gilhooly brothers walked out to the car lot. "By the way, what's your names?"

"Smith," Junior said. "And we're in a hurry."

"Well, let's get down to business then," Timmons said. "We can start the paperwork in my office."

CHAPTER 15

Dwayne Wheeler decided to make another investigative trip through all the counties visited by the burglars. In order not to raise any curiosity he adopted the appearance of a casual citizen. That meant he would have to get replacement license plates for the K.B.I. car since it had the Kansas government type. And he knew a guy who could solve that small problem.

That was Elmer Pettibone.

Pettibone had been the most powerful bootlegger in Wichita during Federal prohibition and the Kansas dry laws. He had a well-organized group of drivers who brought the booze into the state from a secret site during those exciting years. There was a pickup point in Oklahoma near the Texas state line. His best hauler was Dwayne Wheeler. The shamus had a sixth sense when it came to avoiding revenuers' roadblocks and vehicles.

DWAYNE DROPPED DONNA SUE OFF IN FRONT OF the WKH Building the next morning then headed for Mosley Avenue north of Douglas where Elmer Pettibone had a warehouse. When the shamus reached the location, he pulled into the back of the building and parked. Dwayne pushed the doorbell in a pattern of ring, ring-ring, ring and ring-ring-ring. This was the code used for security reasons during prohibition. The shamus knew that his friend was still involved in shady deals that brought him in big bucks.

Dwayne had to wait a few minutes for Elmer to walk from his office to the building's entrance. The rather large portal opened and Dwayne was allowed to enter.

"What's going on, good buddy?" Elmer inquired.

"Big stuff."

Dwayne noticed there was a trio of his old friends playing cards in a corner of the building. They were drivers for Elmer and that meant there was a new racket going on. Dwayne waved and called out, "Hey, guys!"

They looked up and replied with grins. "What're you up to, Dwayne?" one asked.

Dwayne shrugged. "Being a good citizen as always."

The drivers broke out in whoops and one sang out, "None of us are buying that at all!"

The shamus waved back and grinned as he followed Elmer into his office. Elmer invited him to sit down as he went to the filing cabinet and pulled out a pack of cigarettes. "Notice anything unusual about these?"

Dwayne looked, then caught on right away. "They don't have tax labels."

"That's right. I've been in contact with the Dallas bunch and they've invited me to join them in distributing untaxed goodies."

"Interesting."

"Interesting enough to join in?" Elmer asked. "That's what them guys out there have done. But none of 'em can get close to you when it comes to running contraband. So whataya say?"

"I can't. I have a serious caper in the works."

"Well, if you get a hankering for adventure, let me know," Elmer offered. "So what do I owe the pleasure of your visit?"

"I need up-to-date license plates to put on a car," Dwayne said. "I'm planning on doing some snooping around."

"Who're you working for?"

"You ain't gonna believe this, Elmer. I am an official temporary agent of the K.B.I. I need to make an undercover tour of my assignment area."

"Ah! So you want to appear as a civilian, do you?" Elmer remarked. He walked back to the file cabinet and returned with a pair of plates bearing the **SG** of Sedgwick County. "How're these?"

"I'd like a county plate kinda far from here."

Elmer went over to the cabinet and came back with another pair. These had **CN** on them. "This is Cheyenne County. It's way up in the extreme northwest of the state. I think these should suit you."

"Excellent," Dwayne stated. "How much do I owe you?"

"Aw! Take your money and shove it up your ass."

"Thanks a lot, Elmer. I'll have 'em back within a week."

"Take your time. And keep the idea of taxation evasion in your head."

———

DWAYNE HAD DONE SOME COMPLICATED AND dangerous undercover work for the F.B.I. when mobsters from back east suddenly appeared on the Kansas prairie. During the caper he had gone to a thrift shop in Hutchinson to buy some second-hand clothing to be less conspicuous among the locals. He decided to visit that same store to get some clothing. It was located in Reno County where there'd been no burglaries so he could ask questions without arousing suspicion.

The shamus enjoyed the casual drive from Wichita to Hutchinson. He went east on U.S. 54, then turned north on State 17. That took him straight up to the town in question. He rolled slowly along Main Street until sighting the thrift store. After parking at the curb, he left the car and walked through the door. He noticed it had not changed much since he had been there the last time. It was still filled with racks of various styles of clothing. There was also some old furniture off to the side and a counter with kitchenware on display.

A middle-age lady with a kerchief on her head was seated at a battered desk in the back, tending to an inventory notebook. When the woman noticed him, she got up. "Hello there. What can I do for you?"

"Good morning, ma'am," Dwayne said. He saw she was not the same lady who been there when he had made the previous purchases. "I'm on the way to a construction job in Colorado and my work clothes accidently got packed away in a tool crate. I'm gonna have to buy something to wear 'til the duds arrive at the worksite. I don't need nothing too expensive."

"All such clothes are kept along the back wall," the lady said. "Follow me, please."

She took him to the rear of the building where several racks of work clothing were located. "You look around and find what you need. There's a changing room over in the corner if you want to try anything on. I'll be at my desk."

Dwayne began searching through the racks. He picked out a couple of shirts and pants along with a worn fedora and a pair of shoes. There was a stool nearby and he sat down on it to make sure the footwear fit.

After making his choices, he walked over to the changing room and took off his street clothes. The work garments made him appear to be an ordinary traveler. After getting back into his clothes, he walked up to the front of the store.

The lady tallied up three dollars for what he had chosen. Dwayne gave her five and told her to keep the change. She was extremely pleased. "This money you spent will help some of the poorer folks around here. It's operated by our church. I'm one of the volunteers."

"Where do you get the stuff to sell?"

"It's all donations from the congregation. Ever' bit of it. They're very generous."

"They certainly are," Dwayne said. "I've always admired people who have a kindly intent toward those who are more worse off than theirselves."

"It's a shame how some folks find themselves in such bad straits."

"Yeah it sure is," Dwayne agreed. "Well, I'll be off. Thank you kindly."

"Thank *you* kindly, sir!"

———

DWAYNE DROVE SOUTH TO KINGMAN COUNTY TO find a place that might deal with fences. Unfortunately, he didn't find any second-hand stores of any sort. He knew he could cross that place off his list. Next, he continued his southward drive toward the town of Anthony in Harper County. But once more he didn't find anything out of the ordinary.

His final destination was Wellington, the seat of Sumner County. This area was just south of Sedgwick County. It proved to be another disappointment. Now totally pissed off, he decided to stop wasting time and take U.S. 81 to get back to Wichita faster. However, just north of the town of Riverdale, the highway made a sharp change to due east. As he slowed down to make the turn, he noticed a gravel road heading in the opposite direction.

Something kicked up in his shamus psyche, and he made a U-turn, leaving the main highway to follow the gravel route. He felt a dexterous intuition and drove at a steady 35 miles-per-hour for twenty minutes when he came to a crossroads. He slowed down and took note of the location.

There were buildings and structures on three corners of the junction. The largest was a propane gas works across the road where several tanker trucks were parked. Directly opposite that site was a filling station with a large garage to its immediate rear. Electric power lines were strung from a series of poles throughout the area to the various buildings. They were all connected to a main mast standing in the open plot.

A small diner was to his right. Dwayne decided to see what information he could get plus a lunch. He turned around and drove over to the eatery. The interior of the place was simple but clean. There were no booths or tables, just a counter with stools that ran the length of the small structure. He was the only customer and the wait-ress/cook, a heavyset woman with an apron over her dress, gave him a casual greeting. "Howdy. What can I do for you?"

Dwayne looked up at a crudely lettered sign on the wall showing the *carte du jour*.

HAMBURGER...15¢

HOT DOG...10¢

CHILLY...15¢

TATER CHIPS...5¢

POP...5¢

"I'd like a hamburger and tater chips," Dwayne said. "Do you have Orange Crush?"

"I sure do," she assured him. She walked over to a small refrigerator and got the pop, setting it on the counter in front of him. With that done, she tossed him a bag of potato chips and set a bottle of ketchup on the counter. With those preliminaries taken care of, she turned to tend to his order.

After being served, he was surprised at the size and good taste of the hamburger. "Has this area got a name?"

"Not really. Folks just call it Four Corners."

Dwayne glanced out the window as a gasoline tanker truck drove up to the filling station. The big vehicle was obviously going to pump gas into an underground tank. He also noticed several cars in the front and side of the garage.

"Mmm," Dwayne mused, "it seems pretty busy around here."

"Yeah," the woman said. "My husband owns the filling station and garage. His workers always come over here to eat at their lunch hour. That includes the fellers from the propane works."

"I see there's a lot of cars needing service parking around the filling station."

The woman suddenly turned surly. "It's just a plain ol' business for us." Then she walked to the end of the counter, indicating she wasn't in the mood for conversation.

Dwayne's instincts were stimulated by her sudden irritation. He ate slowly, appearing nonchalant and disinterested about where he was. The sound of a vehicle pulling up in front of the café could be heard.

Dwayne turned and looked out the window, seeing a Ford panel truck coming to a stop. The driver, a tall, muscular man got out of his vehicle and entered the diner. He nodded to the woman.

"Hi ya, Wanda. How's about a coupla them hotdogs and a Coke?"

She seemed relieved to see him. "D'you want tater chips with that?"

"You know I don't like chips," he said. "When're you gonna get a fryer to make French fries?"

Wanda grinned at him. "I'll get a fryer as soon as you bring me one." She turned to put two wieners on the grill.

Now Dwayne was completely convinced the area was not on the up-and-up. That meant he had to work out a plan of action.

The man glanced at Dwayne. "How're you doing?"

"Pretty good," the shamus replied. "How're you doing?"

"Perty good. I don't think I've seen you here before."

The woman turned swiftly around and spoke with a tone of warning in her voice. "That's 'cause he ain't never *been* here before."

The man laughed. "Well, welcome to Four Corners."

"Do they have jobs open?"

"I don't know," the man replied. "I just come here to pick up auto parts to take back for my boss."

Dwayne finished eating and left a quarter tip on the counter. "That was a mighty tasty hamburger, Wanda."

"Glad you liked it."

He turned to the man. "Nice talking with you."

"Same here."

Dwayne walked outside, glancing at the panel truck's license plates. They had **RN** on them. Reno County. Dwayne got in his car and headed back toward U.S. 81.

CHAPTER 16

The first thing Dwayne did on the morning of his return from Reno County was to head for Harry Philbin's K.B.I. bailiwick in the City Building. His impatience to meet with Philbin was put to the test when he had to circle the block three times before he found a parking space. With that annoyance taken care of, he hurried up the stairs to the second floor to see Philbin.

The K.B.I. agent was on the phone when Dwayne entered the office and he motioned for the shamus to sit down on a chair in front of his desk. Dwayne complied and bore fifteen frustrating minutes listening to a one-sided telephone call.

When Philbin hung up he gave out a long sigh. "This narcotic operation is turning out to be a combination of confusion and bad leads."

Dwayne responded to the complaint with a quick nod, then stated, "I need a map and aerial photos of Reno County."

"There hasn't been any burglaries there, has there?"

"No. But this caper has gotten more complicated. It's about farmers who are careless locking doors."

Philbin's eyes opened wide with curiosity. "What's happening?"

"I was doing undercover work and found some suspicious activity going on in Reno County. There's a place at a crossroads west of U.S. 81. When I drove to the site I had the feeling all wasn't on the up-and-up at the location. There was a propane plant but wasn't a problem. It was a filling station and garage that bothered me."

Philbin said, "In other words, the site is suspicious."

"Right," Dwayne said. "So I went over to a café across from the garage. When I went in for lunch, I asked the waitress some vague questions about what went on over there. She got huffy and showed a strong inclination of not wanting to talk about the place."

"Did the conversation come to a close?"

"Yeah. But a few minutes later a guy who had pulled up in front of the café walked in and sat down beside me at the counter. He was obviously well known by the woman and she waited on him in a friendly manner."

Now Philbin was very interested.

"The waitress served his lunch then stood behind the counter with her arms folded across a pair of very large boobs. She stared at me with a threatening expression. Naturally I couldn't pursue the subject of the guy's activities. So I made my goodbyes and went out to my car. I noticed the guy's Ford panel truck. It had Reno County plates. I looked across at the filling station again. That's when I noticed stripped down cars behind it."

"Uh huh," Philbin said. "Those were more than likely stolen cars with the parts pulled out of them."

"Yep. And I figured that the guy I saw in the café was taking them someplace in Reno County to be sold."

Philbin nodded his understanding. "Maybe it's in Hutchinson."

"Nope. I've been in Hutchinson a few times and never saw any place that could handle that big an operation. There's obviously a fence operating there, and I figure those burglars take their to loot to that guy."

Philbin got up and went over to a file cabinet. He thumbed through a stash of thick cardboard envelopes and pulled one out. "Here's a map and some aerial photographs of Reno County. We get this information from the Federal Farm Bureau. These statistics are kept up to date, so it's not over three months old. All of the counties in Kansas are covered by that program."

Dwayne took the packet. "Why all the attention?"

"The farmers' planting is limited by the Federal government to avoid over production. But now and then some clodhopper tries to make more money from the harvest by illegally sowing his fields."

The shamus chuckled. "And they accuse Wichitans of being crooked."

"I take it they consider the city a den of vice."

"That's an understatement," Dwayne said, standing got up. "Well, I'm off. I'll be in touch." Dwayne picked up the envelopes. "I hope I can finally dig up some real clues in this caper."

————

DWAYNE WALKED INTO THE OFFICE OF THE Wheeler Detective Agency, hurrying past Donna Sue. "C'mon. I got something to show you. And I'll need some help."

"What's going on?" she asked, following him.

He began explaining the situation as he opened the

packet and laid out the map and photographs. "We need to locate a place that's in Reno County. It'll be an outfit that deals in auto parts taken from stolen cars."

"I thought you were dealing with burglaries of farmhouses."

"I am. But I think that somehow this parts racket is tied in with a gang of thieves."

Donna Sue was confused. "How do you relate one to the other?"

Dwayne tapped his forehead. "It's my professional instinct as a detective, my dear. My brain is burning with curiosity."

He told her about the visit to the road junction and noting the activities—both honest and suspect—at the location. Donna Sue was briefed on the truck driver and his panel truck with the Reno County license plates.

Donna Sue wasn't satisfied. "I still don't see how you connect that with the burglaries."

"The thieves going into the farmers' houses have to get rid of what they steal. They can't take the loot to Pete Driscoll here in Wichita. If there's a place in Reno County that takes parts from stolen cars, it will prob'ly deal in other stuff, too. During my questioning of the farmers, I learned that kitchen appliances seemed to be popular with the burglars."

"But why are you concentrating on that particular county?"

"Because there has been no looting of farm houses in that area."

Donna Sue nodded her head. "Now I see. They don't want the local law to get involved."

"Right. Now let's start scanning the photos."

They settled down, carefully going over the images of

the farmland. It was Donna Sue who struck pay dirt. "Looky here, Dwayne!"

He took the aerial photo she mentioned, and gave it a careful examination. He noticed a narrow dirt pathway leading from a county road. It went across a wooden bridge straddling a creek that led to a spot between two columns of trees. There were two buildings on the site and a near indiscernible barbed wire fence around the entire set up.

"I think this might be it," Dwayne surmised scanning the photograph. "There's a large building that could be a warehouse for storage." He looked closer. "Yeah! There's that panel truck I saw at the crossroads parked in front."

Donna Sue joined him. "And there's also a house behind the warehouse. That must be a dwelling of sorts. See the clothesline back of it?"

"Yeah. Hand me the map, please, sweetie."

He took the chart and laid the photo beside it. "Now I know the exact location."

"I take it you're going out to that spot?"

"Yeah. But I don't want to show up there in daylight. I'll have to go at night. And I'll need you to come along to drive me."

"Does that include me sneaking in there with you?"

"No. But you can stay with the car while I make my one-man reconnaissance into the area. If you see any other vehicles approaching, drive away so they won't notice you parked at night along a county road."

"Good thinking, shamus," Donna Sue said. "Are we going tonight?"

He shook his head. "I've got to write up a report of all this for Harry Philbin to file. We can go tomorrow night."

Donna Sue showed a wide grin. "At last! I can share an adventure with you!"

CHAPTER 17

The Gilhoolys' latest invasion took place in Marion County. This was the farthest north they had traveled during their crime spree. Horatio noticed that his older brothers seemed mysterious on certain occasions. And having the curiosity of a young sibling, he resented being left out of something that was either important or a lot of fun.

Horatio frowned. "I wish I knew what's going on between you two."

"Shut up!" Cornelius said.

"I don't have to if I don't want to."

Cornelius turned around. "You want a bloody nose?"

"No."

"Then keep your yap closed."

Junior slowed down when he sighted a farm house off to their left. He came to a stop when he reached the entrance to a driveway. "It looks like nobody's home."

"I'd say so," Cornelius agreed.

Junior drove up to the back porch where a couple of dogs were lying down. They both looked up with friendly interest at the arrivals. The canines trotted down to the trio with tails wagging. The thieves patted them, then went through a side door to get inside the house.

That particular job yielded some clothing, kitchen utensils, and a jar of dollar bills. The Gilhooly boys patted the dogs again before getting into their car and leaving.

When they were going through a domicile at the next location, Junior was getting tired of hearing Horatio's petulant complaining. "Hey, punk, go out to the barn and see what you can find."

Horatio wasn't pleased. "There won't be anything in a barn that we can put in the luggage rack."

Cornelius glared at him. "You got two choices regarding that damn barn. You can make Junior mad at you or you can stay a happy dipshit."

Horatio, having a little trouble figuring out exactly what Cornelius had just stated, headed for the barn while his two older brothers went into the house. They found various items, gathered them up and went outside to the car. The one first-time article they had stolen was a barber kit complete with electric shaver, moustache comb and both pre- and after-shave lotions.

When they walked out of the house, the older siblings saw Horatio standing behind the car with a big grin on his face. Junior walked up to the youngster. "What're you so happy about?"

"Look in the luggage rack."

Junior did as requested, then broke out with a delighted laugh. "Come here, Corny, and take a gander at this."

Horatio had taken a toolbox from the barn to the car and put it in the luggage rack. The lid was open, displaying an array of expensive hand tools.

Junior was impressed. "Wow! We'll keep this for ourselves."

"Yeah!" Cornelius agreed. "We can use it to work on the Oldsmobile."

"What Oldsmobile?" Horatio asked.

Junior glared at Cornelius, saying, "Yeah! What Oldsmobile, Corny?"

Cornelius realized he had betrayed the secret scheme between himself and Junior. "Well...uh...uh...if we was to ever buy an Oldsmobile, we'd use these tools to keep it running."

Horatio was excited. "Are we going to purchase an Oldsmobile?"

Junior patted him on the shoulder. "When we're able to buy another car, it'll be an Oldsmobile." He turned to Cornelius. "Ain't that right?"

"It sure is. You bet your ass."

"C'mon," Junior said. "We got time for one more job."

———

IT WAS ONE A.M. WHEN DWAYNE BROUGHT THE K.B.I. car to a halt on the country road. He and Donna Sue looked in the glow of the headlights and spotted an opening in the barbed wire fence. It was an entrance to a narrow trail that could be seen fading out of sight in the gloom.

"This is it," Dwayne said. "See that bridge over there? That's where the creek must be." He looked at the map one more time, then said, "Okay. I'm ready to go."

"Don't forget that steak," Donna Sue reminded him.

"I'm glad you suggested a big one," Dwayne said,

switching off the headlights. "There might be more'n one dog."

Dwayne got out of the car, allowing Donna Sue to slide across the seat to settle behind the wheel. He had a flashlight and his Colt semi-automatic pistol with a couple of extra magazines of .45 caliber bullets. He looked up at the sky. "Not many clouds, but I'm glad there's not a full moon. I'm taking enough of a chance with this flashlight if I need it."

"Be real careful," Donna Sue urged.

"I will. And you remember to drive away if you see any approaching cars."

"Right. But I don't think country people go out this late at night."

Dwayne walked rapidly across the road to the opening in the barbed wire and continued toward the bridge. A small creek gurgled underneath it as he crossed to where the trail began. He noticed a lot of tire tracks as he approached the trees ahead. The shamus entered the two columns of elms and made his way down to a spot where he could see the warehouse. A dog barked when he was adjacent to the structure. Now he pulled the T-bone steak from the sack he carried. The dog barked again, this time closer.

Dwayne was surprised the animal was not more aggressive when it trotted toward to him. The noise it made was more of curiosity than threat. When it appeared from the darkness, he could see it was a mixed breed of perhaps a golden retriever and a boxer.

"Here, boy! Here, boy!"

Dwayne knelt down and held out the steak. The dog wasted no time in figuring out he was about to be fed. The canine hurried over and took the meat. With that done, the shamus made his way onto the site where three vehicles were parked. When he drew closer he recognized the panel truck the guy at the café had been driving. He checked the license to make sure it was the same. He was pleased to finally discern that his idea of the guy's connections was correct. Next he checked the windows in the warehouse finding two on either side of the door.

Now Dwayne used the flashlight and shined it into the interior of the building. He saw kitchenware, clothing and crates of various sizes that he figured held automobile parts. It was more proof that this site had strong ties with the one in Sumner County called Four Corners.

He prowled around the area for ten minutes, making mental notes of the layout. Satisfied, he headed back toward the road. He met the dog again, who wagged his tail and accompanied him out of the column for trees. Dwayne patted the canine once more before continuing the short trek.

Donna Sue scooted back to the passenger's side of the car. "What'd you find?"

"That place plays a big role in the caper," Dwayne stated as he started the car. "And it looks like I'm going to get a hold of that guy with the panel truck and wring some info out of him."

"I wouldn't be too threatening," Donna Sue warned.

"Okay," the shamus said. "I'll be real nice." He stepped on the accelerator and headed down the road, happily anticipating coming events.

CHAPTER 18

I t was Sunday morning when Tommy Brady turned his pickup truck into the parking lot of the Methodist Church in the town of Augusta. When he first woke up that morning, he felt a cold coming on, but figured it would clear up eventually.

Now, however, the soreness in his throat had begun to sharpen, and he coughed a couple of times. He looked upward, saying, "Well, Lord, you'll have to excuse me, but I don't think I better go inside your house to worship this morning. There ain't any sense in giving other folks a cold. Amen!" Then he added, "I pray, Lord, that you don't let this one turn into the flu. Amen again!"

He turned around and headed back to his farmhouse. During the short drive back, more symptoms came up causing coughing and the beginning of a headache. When he pulled into his driveway and reached the house, he was surprised to see a Model A Ford parked by the kitchen entrance.

He got out of his pickup and walked through the door. He was confronted by three young men who were obviously stealing objects and putting them on the kitchen table to take out. Tommy, a forgiving Christian, cleared his throat and said, "Say, fellers, you—"

Cornelius pulled his .38 snub-nose revolver from his waist holster and fired it twice. Both bullets slammed into Tommy's chest. The old man was thrown back against the wall by the double impacts and slumped down to the floor.

Horatio was shocked. "Oh, Corny! What have you done?"

Junior hurried over and knelt down by the victim. "Aw, man! He ain't breathing and his eyes is open but he ain't blinking." He looked over at Cornelius. "What the fuck did you do that for?"

Cornelius was about to hyperventilate as he replaced his pistol in the holster. "Uh...uh...the guy surprised...he surprised me...that's what he done."

"Well, you kilt him dead, "Junior growled, then had a second thought. "It's good he ain't alive. That's good, all right. He can't do no talking." He got to his feet. "Let's get the hell outta here!"

The three Gilhoolys grabbed their booty and rushed from the house to their car.

———

JUST AS DWAYNE AND DONNA SUE ENTERED their office on Monday morning, the phone began ringing. Donna Sue quickly answered it. "Wheeler Detective Agency. Where may I direct your call?" A quick moment passed, then she handed the handset to Dwayne. "It's Bobby Terwilliger."

"Hey, Bobby," Dwayne said. "How's the *Wichita Eagle's* ace crime reporter?"

"I got bad news, Dwayne. I'm afraid your friend Tommy Brady was murdered sometime yesterday."

It took a moment for Dwayne to reply. "Aw, shit! Don't tell me that, Bobby!"

"It happened in his house near Augusta. The kitchen had been stripped of utensils. It was obviously a burglary gone bad. The case has been turned over to the Highway Patrol. George Madison at the Wichita office here is in charge if you want any information."

"Thanks...thanks, Bobby." Dwayne hung up the phone and turned to Donna Sue who sensed something awful had happened. "Tommy was murdered yesterday."

"Oh, Dwayne! No!"

Dwayne, badly confused, took breaths. A moment longer, those breaths turned to sobs. Donna Sue walked up and bent down, putting her arm around him. "I know how terrible this is for you, dearest Dwayne. And I feel awful, too."

Dwayne continued weeping for the loss of a friend who had been so kind to him and his mother.

———

IN THE EARLY AFTERNOON, DWAYNE HAD recovered enough to make an official call on Captain George Madison who was in charge of Troop F of the Kansas Highway Patrol in Wichita. The two men were casual acquaintances from having met on law enforcement activities several times over the years.

Dwayne had a briefcase with him when he walked through the door. The captain was surprised when the shamus displayed a K.B.I. badge. Dwayne spoke in a strained voice. "Bobby Terwilliger of the *Eagle* told me about the murder of Tommy Brady at his home. He was a close friend of mine."

"Sorry for your loss. What can I do for you?"

"I'm working on some burglaries that occurred in farm houses in several counties. I think Tommy's murder was part of those crimes. Maybe we can help each other out."

"That would certainly be convenient," Madison said. "But it sounds like you're already involved in it."

Dwayne pulled a packet of papers out of the briefcase. "These are my notes on the case that might help you guys if the Highway Patrol is gonna solve Tommy's death."

"I suppose we will, but that's not a certainty."

"You'll see that all the crimes were committed on Sunday mornings. That's exactly what happened to Tommy."

Madison nodded. "That's correct according to what the Butler County sheriff's report indicated."

"It seems that farmers aren't much on locking their doors when they leave their houses to go to church on Sunday," Dwayne said. "That's when the burglars enter the homes. I learned that during my own investigation. I questioned a boy who had stayed home from church. He said three guys came into the house. They were surprised to see him, then asked for directions to Harper. They were all young men. Their descriptions are in my reports. Unfortunately, the kid didn't get a look at their car."

"Have there been any other shootings or assaults?"

"Yeah," Dwayne replied. "An old man was punched in the face. And he's blind, so he didn't see the burglars but he sensed there were three of 'em."

"I'll pass all this off to my investigation team," Madison said, setting the papers aside. "So you're not a private eye any more, huh?"

"This K.B.I. is a temporary situation since they're loaded down with narcotics cases."

"It's a growing problem, all right. We catch a couple of users now and then when they're pulled over for speeding or other reasons. But so far the pushers haven't made any appearances."

Dwayne stood up. "I'm taking a personal interest in Tommy's murder. So if you need any sensitive actions to be taken, let me know. That'll leave you guys in the clear."

Madison knew that meant Dwayne would break the law when interrogating suspects who were reluctant to cooperate.

"Take it easy, Dwayne. Don't do anything that'll get you in trouble."

———

LILLY GILHOOLY WAS HYSTERICAL WHEN SHE learned that her son Cornelius had committed murder. They fearfully avoided telling her about the crime until Tuesday morning when they all sat around the kitchen table. The revelation set her off in a panicky state and she bawled them out for the crime that could be linked to them.

Junior interrupted her wailings. "Listen, Ma. Don't get so worked up. The guy was dead before he hit the floor. So he can't tell nobody nothing. We had already gathered up what he had worth stealing. It was all on the table. We took it with us so's they couldn't find any fingerprints."

It took five minutes for Lilly to calm down enough to speak. "That was a good idea. I mean about the finger-prints. You and Cornelius would have been found out since you got prison records."

"Sure," Junior said. "We don't have nothing to worry about."

"Well, there's one thing you're gonna do," Lilly said. "You take whatever you got from that house and bury it. You understand? *Bury it*! We don't want nothing to link us up with a killing."

Junior turned to Horatio. "You heard what Ma said. There's a shovel on the back porch."

Lilly interrupted. "Wait a minute, Junior! Horatio ain't gonna do no digging. In fact, he ain't going out with you and Cornelius no more. Understand?"

"Okay, Ma," Junior replied. He motioned to Cornelius. "Since you did the killing, you can get the shovel to dig."

CHAPTER 19

Dwayne's grief went through various moods after Tommy's death. At times he was in a relatively calm state of mind, then within thirty minutes or an hour he lapsed back into spasms of sadness and a keen sense of loss.

Donna Sue could see there was a very strong possibility he might sink into a long intense depression. A couple of evenings after the tragedy, she soothed him as they sat together in their bedroom. Dwayne was lying on the bed, not moving, just staring up at the ceiling. Donna Sue sat down beside him. She spoke in a soothing voice, suggesting that he remain at home until he felt better. He agreed and she left him to go to the office to handle phone calls and inform potential clients that Detective Wheeler would not be available until further notice.

———

THREE DAYS PASSED AND DWAYNE HAD FINALLY developed complete control over his sorrow. He told

Donna Sue he had everything under control and wanted get back on the caper. He still had the license plates he'd gotten from Elmer Pettibone.

Dwayne dropped off Donna Sue at the W.K.H. Building, then headed for a confab with Harry Philbin. He knew he would have some explaining to do when he stepped into the man's office.

When he arrived he found that the K.B.I. supervisor had been so busy on the narcotics campaign that he hadn't noticed Dwayne's absence. Philbin looked up at the shamus' unexpected presence. "Ah! I haven't been able to give you a call to see how things are going. I'm being slammed by running other assignments and details on the narcotics situation."

"Well, there was another appearance by those burglars," Dwayne informed him. "This time in Butler County. And it included a murder. The victim was my best friend."

Philbin stopped what he was doing and gazed carefully at Dwayne across his desk. "You seem a bit out of sorts. And I'm aware of the crime."

"I got things under control," Dwayne assured him. "Don't worry none about that."

"Okay. The reason I know of the homicide was because the Highway Patrol has passed the case over to us. This was after you visited Captain Madison at the Wichita headquarters."

"That's good news. I got a score to settle."

Philbin was concerned. "Listen up, Dwayne! You can't carry on this assignment like a private investigator. You're K.B.I. now. Keep that in mind. You got to stick to the law."

"Sure."

Philbin opened a desk drawer and pulled out a folder. "This is the Highway Patrol's report along with the Butler County sheriff's."

Dwayne took the document and left the office, driving directly back to Donna Sue at the W.K.H. Building. His sudden appearance surprised her. He held up the case documents given him by Philbin. "C'mon. Let's both of us go over this."

"What've you got there, Dwayne?"

"The Highway Patrol has passed Tommy's murder over me to handle since it is tied up to the burglaries."

They sat down at his desk and Dwayne pulled out the packet. The first thing they saw was highly disturbing for both of them. It was a photo of Tommy showing him lying dead in his kitchen. His eyes were open but sunken in death and his mouth had twisted into a grimace.

Dwayne turned his attention to the autopsy report that was short and to the point. It was a homicide caused by two gunshot wounds. Both were lethal. The rest of the report was the usual information about gender, age, appearance, etc. Dwayne sighed. "I guess Tommy is a statistic now."

Donna Sue patted his hand. "Let's go over the investigative report."

The information was sketchy. The house had been dusted for fingerprints, but none were found except Tommy's. There were narrow tracks in the dirt driveway outside that indicated an old vehicle had been there. Other tracks were from the local farmers who passed by to drive out to work their rented land.

Dwayne wasn't completely satisfied. "I think we should go out there and take a look around."

———

WHEN THEY ARRIVED AT THE FARMHOUSE THEY noted a pickup truck parked by the side entrance. As they got out of the car, two teenage boys appeared with the kitchen table, putting it into the back of the truck.

"Hey!" Dwayne yelled. "What the hell do you think you're doing!"

The bigger of the two looked over and frowned at him. "That's none of your business."

"Yeah," his skinny companion added.

Dwayne walked rapidly over to the husky kid. He displayed his K.B.I. badge and growled, "Put that fucking table back into that fucking house. What you're doing is a criminal act."

The kid was obviously taken aback. "I'm Don Thompson. My Aunt Margie lived here with her husband Uncle Tommy. That is to say, Tom Brady."

Dwayne relaxed as Donna Sue joined them. "Okay, Don. But you can't take anything out of the house for two reasons. First, it's still a crime scene. And, second, Tommy left all his possessions to the Wichita Salvation Army. I know that for a fact since I witnessed the will when he signed it."

"Okay," Don said. "I thought it would be okay if I took some things that me and my pal here could use."

"Yeah," Skinny said. He paused and offered his hand. "I'm Jerry Roberts."

Dwayne now could tell they were a couple of polite kids. "Glad to meet you. I'm Dwayne Wheeler and this is my wife Donna Sue."

"Wow!" Jerry exclaimed. "You're *that* detective!"

"Yeah. I'm *that* detective."

Donna Sue entered the conversation, quickly explaining the case that Dwayne was working on. She concluded, "He was doing all the investigations at the places where the burglaries occurred. Tommy was his best friend and Dwayne is going to find his killers if he has to go to the ends of the earth."

Don spoke up. "Both me and Jerry knew him really well. He was a religious guy but he didn't throw it in your face. He was on the county park committee and organized a lot of athletics. He had been a boxer in the Navy."

"How old are you guys?" Dwayne asked.

"We're both twenty," Jerry replied "We left our family farms to break into the stockcar races held up at Newton. We live in an old house on the edge of town getting ready for the races."

"Yeah," Don said. "We've got a '32 Pontiac to get ready for action. The local feed store, barbershop and the Conoco station are sponsoring us. The two of us have been saving up money for this since we was in junior high school."

"It's kind of embarrassing for us to be caught taking stuff out of his house, but we're short on cash," Jerry said.

"By the way we'd like to help you out if you could use us," Don informed him. "So if we can do anything for you, just give us a call." He pulled a business card out of his shirt pocket. "You can reach us here and we always have some time to spare."

Dwayne knew that would never happen, but he appreciated their offer. "Yeah. I'll get in touch with you." He winked at them. "Will you please return the table to the kitchen?"

"You bet we will, Mister Wheeler."

Dwayne helped them get the piece of furniture out of their pickup truck. "Well, I hope you have good luck in your races."

"Thank you," they both said in unison.

"Be careful on that race track," Donna Sue said.

The boys got in the pickup truck and drove off the property. Dwayne turned and looked at the farmhouse for a few moments. Then he and Donna Sue left the site.

CHAPTER 20

Tommy Brady's funeral service was held at the Methodist Church. The mourners, besides Dwayne and Donna Sue, were the members of the church congregation. Other attendees were farm families who rented land from Tommy, town acquaintances and Salvation Army soldiers from Wichita. The latter were a trio of a guitarist, violinist and guitar.

The pastor gave a sermon regarding Tommy's deep faith and devotion as a Christian. "Tommy had a friend who was particularly close to him. That was Dwayne Wheeler. We all know of Dwayne's service to the community as a law enforcer. He requested a chance to tell us of Tommy's Christian mercy."

Dwayne walked up to the pulpit, turned and took a deep breath. He wasn't much of a speaker, so Donna Sue had typed up a simple oration that told of the kindness Tommy had shown his mother and him and the departed's true dedication to his Christian faith. Dwayne also pointed out Tommy's sense of humor and friendliness. His voice broke a couple of times during the delivery, but he managed to speak all the way to the finish.

At the end of the pastor's sermon and prayers, the Salvation Army musicians performed *Amazing Grace, Rock of Ages* and *Onward Christian Soldiers*. The congregation joined in with the singing.

After the services, Tommy's pallbearers carried him from the church to the hearse. These were Dwayne, Jerry Roberts, Don Thompson and three laymen. A parade of cars and pickup trucks made up the followers.

Tommy was buried next to Margie in the Thompson family cemetery a few yards in back of the barn. The two stockcar racers Don and Jerry had come to the site the day before to dig the grave.

After the small crowd withdrew, Don and Jerry filled in the grave with Dwayne's help. When the chore was finished, the two young men nodded a goodbye to Dwayne and Donna Sue.

The couple went straight back to the apartment house from the funeral. She was glad Dwayne had now gotten complete control over his emotions from Tommy's death. However, she was worried about what violent actions he might take if and when he came into contact with the murderers.

After arriving home, Dwayne suggested they should sit down on the sofa to discuss the present circumstances. When he spoke, it was obvious he had given the matter some serious thought. "I think that place called the Four Corners west of Highway 81 has some contacts with this situation. And by that, I mean Tommy's death."

She nodded her agreement. "Good thought. It's obvious they have connections with that place in Reno County."

"When I looked in the warehouse I knew they were

not only dealing with parts from stolen cars. I saw kitchen appliances, clothing and other stuff that was more'n likely burglarized in those farm houses. The guy who picks up stuff at the Four Corners takes the car parts to the Reno County location. Maybe he knows something about the gang who robs farmhouses. And I have no doubt they're the ones who killed Tommy." He paused for a thoughtful moment. "I just got an idea!"

"And what is that idea?"

"I'm going to Four Corners on Friday. That's the day he comes to pick up the auto parts. I'll ask him if he knows where I can unload some goods."

"I don't quite follow you," Donna Sue said. "What sort of goods?"

Dwayne shook his head. "It's best if I don't tell you."

Now she was certain Dwayne's emotional state had eased into a mood of cold, calculating anger. "Dwayne Wheeler! You better not get into any trouble!"

————

THE NEXT MORNING DWAYNE MADE ANOTHER call on Elmer Pettibone at his warehouse. Elmer answered the doorbell and gave his old comrade-in-liquor-runs a happy grin. "Are you ready to work for me again, Dwayne?"

"Sort of," Dwayne answered.

"Well, let's go to my office and do some palavering," Elmer suggested.

After the pair settled down around Elmer's desk, he asked, "What d'you have in mind?"

"I want to haul some of your samples."

"Samples of what?"

"Tax-free cigarettes," Dwayne replied.

"Whoa there, partner! Don't forget that's a K.B.I. vehicle even if it's got a Cheyenne license plate on it!"

"I ain't talking about during one of your runs with it," Dwayne explained.

Elmer frowned. "Looky here now, Dwayne. You ain't making sense."

Dwayne took a deep breath. "I need to use them cigarettes to sneak into a couple of places. One is an outfit that strips down stolen cars and the other is a big outfit that fences stolen goods."

Elmer pulled a cigar from his shirt pocket. He bit off the end and lit it. "What in the blue-eyed world does that have to do with illegal cigarettes?"

Dwayne knew he wasn't doing very well explaining his plan. "Okay, okay, Elmer. I want to break up a gang that goes around robbing farmhouses. They're the bunch of low-life bastards that killed Tommy Brady."

"Mmm," Elmer mused. "I read about that in the *Eagle*."

"The only way I can get close enough to nab them burglars is to work my way into a car parts outfit that fences stolen goods, see? They're the guys that know where the bunch that killed Tommy are located."

Elmer looked deep into Dwayne's eyes. "Uh huh."

"I know a guy that hauls stolen stuff for the car guys. I want to show him illegal cigarettes in the trunk of the car I'm using. Then I'm going to ask him if he will take me to his boss to see if he would be inter'sted in buying the cigarettes to sell. I'm pretty certain he'll take that bait. Then I'll eventually run into the burglary gang."

"And you arrest or shoot 'em, right?"

"There ain't gonna be any arrests," Dwayne said in a cold tone of voice.

Elmer sighed. "I can't figure all that out, but I know

for a fact that you're a slick son of a bitch, Dwayne Wheeler." He stood up. "C'mon, I'll get you a single box load of illegal cigarettes.

———

IT WAS FRIDAY MORNING AND DWAYNE WAS parked at the intersection of U.S. 81 and the gravel road that led to the site called Four Corners. He was far enough off the junction that the truck driver would not see him when he passed by on his routine errand to pick up automobile parts.

The shamus sat on the fender of the car, patiently waiting for his quarry. He had to piss several times but he didn't have to use bottles like he did during detective capers. The morning slowly faded away until the sun was almost directly over his head.

Another hour passed and the Ford panel truck suddenly came into view. Dwayne watched the vehicle leave the highway and kick up dust. He waited for fifteen minutes to roll by so he wouldn't appear to be following closely.

When he pulled up in front of the diner, he nonchalantly got out of his car and walked through the door. He stopped and looked at the driver. "Hey! It's you. D'you remember me?"

Clemens grinned. "Sure I do. I don't know your name though."

"Dwayne. Just plain Dwayne."

"I'm Jeb. What're you doing in these parts?"

"I remember the big juicy hamburger I got here."

Wanda the waitress showed a grin. She liked being complemented. "You want Orange Crush with that hamburger?"

"You got that right," Dwayne said, sitting on a stool.

Wanda gave Jeb a couple of hot dogs and a coke, then turned to take care of Dwayne's order.

Jeb took a big bite, then asked, "What kind a work are you in, Dwayne?"

"I got a box of samples I picked up in Dallas. I'm anxious to make connections to haul 'em up through Kansas to the Canadian border."

Wanda set the hamburger and soda pop in front of Dwayne.

Clemens was curious. "What do you haul, Dwayne? If you don't mind telling me."

"Well...it's sort of...well..."

Now Jeb laughed. "Don't be shy with me. I'm dealing in lots of stuff that ain't exactly on the legal side."

Wanda glared at him. "Watch what you're saying, Jeb!"

"I tell you what," Dwayne said. "After we finish this scrumptious lunch, I'll take you out to my car and show you my goods."

Small talk died down as the men ate. Wanda was obviously nervous and had a semi-scowl on her face. Dwayne swallowed his last drop of Orange Crush and stood up.

"C'mon, Jeb."

The two went out to Dwayne's car. He reached in his pocket and pulled out his keys. After a glance around, he opened the trunk to reveal a cardboard box he got from Elmer Pettibone. "You want to know what's in there, Jeb?"

"Sure."

"Cigarettes."

"Cigarettes?" Jeb asked showing disappointment. "What's so illegal about that?"

Dwayne reached down in the trunk and picked up a

box-cutter. He sliced open the box, pulled out a carton of cigarettes and showed them to Jeb. "What do you think this is?"

Jeb shrugged. "Chesterfield cigarettes, that's what it is."

"Take another look."

"It's a just a pack of Chesterfields," Jeb repeated.

"Don't you see something special? There ain't a blue tax stamp on the top."

"Oh, yeah!" Jeb exclaimed.

"I'm working for an outfit that peddles these cigarettes, man! These here are samples of what can be sold without Federal tax. We charge five cents a pack."

"How much do your customers sell 'em for?" Jeb asked.

"They set their own prices. But it's a hell of a good profit."

Jeb's mind turned over fast. "I got a good idea, Dwayne. I'll be going back to my place of business today after getting the automobile parts. I'll tell my boss about these cigarettes and see if he's inter'sted."

"Good!" Dwayne said. "Where will we be going?"

"I can't take you there now, but there's a nice motor court this side of Hutchinson for you to stay tonight. It's called the Happy Traveler Motor Court. There's running water, carports and a pay phone just outside the lobby. Plus a nice café close by. I'll go see my boss and get back to you."

Dwayne held out his hand. "I'll be waiting, Jeb. By the way my last name is Thompson.

"Mine is Clemens."

CHAPTER 21

Maybelle Gilhooly was getting along quite well using the makeup lessons given her by Lydia Graham. Donna Sue Wheeler visited her as often as possible and was happily surprised to see that her stages of appearance were improving. At first she had gone slowly from plain to cute, and she continued improve faster until she was finally an attractive grown-up woman.

There were others also noticing her good looks. These admirers were the male employees of Whitaker's Laundry. All the young women were leery of each and every one of them. These were middle-aged supervisors who were all grandfathers over 50 years of age.

The foreman of the laundry room was an unpleasant man by the name of Earl. This middle-age man was bald with strands of hair combed across his bare head. He had a stale body odor, bad breath and an irritating habit of patting the girls' fannies as he walked past them.

When Earl noticed Maybelle's blossoming good looks, he began giving her a lot of unwanted attention. He went so far as to hint that if Maybelle was "nice" to him, he could get her a raise in pay and the choice of any day off she wanted. Maybelle had to be careful and she silently ignored the offerings. Earl decided to give her Sundays off in the hopes she would eventually be "nice" to him.

The delivery truck drivers were younger, but their looks were not enough for her to want any dates with them. The married drivers admired her from a distance and the bachelors all made passes at Maybelle now and then. Each time one winked or gave her lewd looks, she shuddered at their unwanted attention.

———

ONE FRIDAY, MAYBELLE AND SALLY DUNCAN were working on the same washing machine together, when Sally gave Maybelle a grin. "Have you seen him?"

"Seen who?"

"The new driver that was just hired," Sally said. "All the girls are going crazy over him."

"I doubt that."

"Oh, yeah! I seen him myself during a break. And he's a dreamboat. *A dreamboat!*"

Maybelle shrugged. "Keep him for yourself then."

"I wish I could," Sally said, throwing sheets into the washing machine. "*He is a dreamboat!*"

———

WHEN THE FRIDAY QUITTING BELL BEGAN ringing, Maybelle and Sally wound up their work, then went to the cloakroom to clock out. Sally got her coat out of the locker and looked over at Maybelle. "There's some shopping I want to take care of."

"Okay. I'll see you later."

Maybelle went out the back entrance when one of the delivery trucks pulled up. The driver stepped down from the cab and nodded to her, "Hi, there."

She stopped short. "Hi."

"I'm new here," he said, offering a hand. "Johnny Lewis."

"I'm Maybelle Gilhooly." She thought he was the handsomest male she had ever laid eyes on. He had a clean-cut look with black hair, blue eyes and an athletic build.

"I just got out of the army. I drove a truck in a transportation unit for three years, so I thought I'd stick to that until I found something else in civilian life. I went through the want-ads of the *Wichita Eagle*. And, whattaya know! Whitaker's Laundry needed a delivery truck driver." He chuckled. "So here I am."

"Yes you are."

He paused a moment. "I don't want to be rude or nothing, but are you attached to somebody? I noticed you don't have a wedding ring." He shrugged. "I don't mean to be nosey."

Normally she would have turned down a quick request for a date like that. Maybelle surprised herself when she accepted. "Uh...no. I ain't married or nothing like that. No boyfriends or anything."

"Actually I don't have nobody to go with either," Johnny said. "Wichita is my hometown, but my girlfriend sent me a Dear-John letter while I was in the army."

"Oh? What's a Dear-John letter?"

"She found somebody else," Johnny said. "And my folks have retired and moved to southern Texas. That leaves me pretty much on my own here in Wichita."

"I reckon so."

"Uh...would you like to take in a movie or something

on Saturday night. There's a good'un at the Miller. It's a Randolph Scott western called *Gunfighters*."

"Yes. I'd like that a lot."

"Hey! We can take in dinner beforehand."

"That would be nice," Maybelle said.

"Do you like Mexican food?

She shrugged. "I ain't never had any of that."

"Well take it from me it's really swell," Johnny said. "My folks moved where they'd have a warm climate along with Mexican food. There's a Mexican restaurant on East Kellogg. It's called the El Charro Café."

"That sounds exciting."

"I guess that means you want to go," Johnny said.

"Yes."

"We ought to start the evening about five o'clock. Is that all right?"

"It'll be real nice...Johnny."

"I got to go in and check out now. Then I could drive you home to find out where you live."

"My home is the Randall Hotel a couple of blocks from here."

"Okay," Johnny said with a grin. "I'll be right back."

She waited for ten minutes, then he returned. "C'mon, Maybelle. My faithful old Dodge is out in the parking lot just waiting to give us a ride."

———

IT WAS EVENING AND DONNA SUE SAT ON THE sofa with an unread magazine in her lap. She was worried about Dwayne. She knew that he was into something risky when he wouldn't tell her his exact plan in this latest caper. Dwayne's background had startled her on more than one occasion. She knew about his former life betting on the horses, bootlegging and some outright dangerous things with Pete Van Dyke, his old commanding officer in the army.

The phone rang and she got up and hurried over to the kitchen counter. "Hello."

"Hi, sweetie, it's me."

"At last! What's been going on?"

"Well," Dwayne said, "you're not going to believe what I'll be doing."

"Try me."

"Remember that night recon we made? I'll be going back there, but this time by invitation. I got things set up to check out those burglars who will be bringing in their loot to sell. And those will be the ones who killed Tommy."

"Are you sure they'll be the right ones?"

"Those'll be who I'm looking for if they've got a lot of kitchen utensils."

"Please be careful, Dwayne. You'll be all alone."

"I admit I don't know exactly how to deal with 'em right now, but I can figure a way to get the job done when they're within my reach."

"Where are you right now, Dwayne?"

"I'm staying at a motor court just south of Hutchinson. I'm talking to you from a public phone booth outside the office."

"I want to go up there to be with you."

"Forget it. Your presence would make things even more risky. Okay? Bye."

"Bye."

Now, more worried than ever, Donna Sue hung up, knowing she was going to have some sleepless nights.

CHAPTER 22

It was a quiet mid-morning and Dwayne Wheeler lay on the bed in the Happy Traveler Motor Court. He waited with a detective's patience for the planned visit of Jeb Clemens.

The ashtray on the bedstand was overrun with cigarette butts next to a radio that was playing the latest country-western songs. The shamus expected it wouldn't be long for Jeb to come and fetch him to meet his boss. Whoever that guy was, Dwayne was sure he would be curious about the money-making smuggling of untaxed cigarettes.

The sound of a motor coming to a stop outside caught Dwayne's attention. He got off the bed and peered through the window. Jeb Clemens stepped out of his panel truck and walked toward the cabin.

The shamus opened the door and admitted Clemens into the room. "How's things going, Jeb?"

"Pretty good, Dwayne. My boss was hesitant at first, but I convinced him to let you explain how your gang does their business. I told him that dealing with illegal cigarettes was a lot like prohibition."

"Sure. I was expecting he would want some lowdown on the racket."

"Okay. C'mon and I'll drive you out to see him."

Dwayne shook his head. "No way. I don't leave my car for any reason. This is a big operation that will stretch from Louisiana all the way up into the Canadian border. So I'll be following you in my car."

Jeb was quiet for a few moments, then he cleared his throat. "Okay. I'll drive back and give him the word."

"Can't you call him?"

"I'm afraid there ain't a telephone out there."

Dwayne lit another Lucky Strike. "If you ain't back by six o'clock, I'll figure the guy ain't interested."

Jeb left the room and got back into his truck. Dwayne stood in the door watching him drive away. He knew that if he showed hesitation and suspicion, it would mean he was in a high class racket. The shamus had dealt with so many crooks—especially the greedy ones—that he was confident Jeb would be back.

Dwayne felt the pangs of hunger, so he got the keys to the K.B.I. car and drove from the Happy Traveler Motor Court over to a nearby drive-in. He bought a cheese-burger, chocolate milkshake and French fries to go. He returned to the motor court and settled down to consume the food. He ate slowly, hoping that everything would work without any hitches.

A half hour later, the motor of Jeb's truck sounded outside and the shamus knew his plan of attack would soon be a reality. There was a knock on the door and Dwayne called out, "C'mon in, Jeb."

Jeb came in with a look of satisfaction. "My boss is willing to hear what you have to offer."

"Okay. Let me finish my French fries."

———

DWAYNE FOLLOWED JEB'S PANEL TRUCK DOWN to the entrance into the compound. As he drew closer he saw that the warehouse looked much bigger in sunlight than it had when he snuck in during those dark hours. Jeb pulled up to the door and stopped. Dwayne parked and got out of the car to join him.

A dog appeared from nowhere and ran up to Dwayne. He realized this was the one he had given a steak. The animal wagged his tail and looked up at the shamus with canine adoration.

"Friendly, huh?" Dwayne said, petting him.

Jeb was surprised. "He generally ain't this fond of strangers."

"Dogs have always liked me."

They entered the large building where shelves were arranged across the width of the room. Dwayne could see auto parts, clothing and household goods. He made a mental note of the merchandise. There was also the sound of out-of-sight masculine voices in the back. To the shamus there seemed to be three men and they were doing some buying and selling.

"Shorty!" Jeb yelled out.

A small man appeared from the back shelves. He was dressed in a denim shirt and bib overalls. He spoke to Jeb in a gravelly voice. "Is this the cigarette feller?"

"This is him, Shorty. Name of Dwayne." He turned to the shamus. "Dwayne, this here is Shorty."

"Howdy," Dwayne said. He could see that the little guy was adroit and sharp in spite of his tacky and loutish appearance.

Shorty shifted a wad of tobacco in his mouth from one side to the other. "Let's go over to the house."

He led the way out of the warehouse and walked toward the dwelling with Dwayne and Jeb following. When they reached the front door, Shorty entered first without knocking. Dwayne saw a plump woman with red hair in the austere parlor.

Shorty spoke up, "Dwayne, this here's my wife Katy."

"How do you do, Katy?"

She ignored the greeting. "There's coffee on the kitchen stove. Help yourself." With that, she went into the back room.

Jeb got three cups from the counter and poured the brew and brought them over to the scratched-up dining table. Shorty gave Dwayne a suspicious look. "Tell me about this here cigarette thing."

"The organization I'm part of has a source of untaxed cigarettes," Dwayne began. "Our plans are to build up a distribution of them from New Orleans to the Canadian border. Right now we've reached Oklahoma City. My boss wanted me to find a spot in the middle of Kansas. And this place fills the bill. That's why I'm here."

"How did you hear about me?" Shorty asked.

"I met Jeb in the café down at Four Corners," Dwayne said. "I guess you know where it's located."

Shorty shook his head. "I never been there."

"I see. Well, anyhow, me and Jeb was eating lunch in the café, and we got to talking and I found out he was hauling car parts from there up to here. One thing led to another about his deliveries. This place seemed to offer security from the law, so I let Jeb in on what I was doing."

Shorty leaned back in his chair. "How many of them cigarettes do you ship at one time?"

"A thousand cartons."

Shorty was thoughtful for a couple of moments. "How often?"

"Four times a month," Dwayne said.

"How'm I gonna do that? I ain't got no trucks."

"We're furnishing the trucks," Dwayne explained, "and we need you to have a place for a change of drivers. I figure that Jeb can fill that bill. He can drive up to the Canadian border, then turn around and drive the truck back to the other driver who'll head back down south for another load. Jeb would still have time to pick up the auto parts."

"And how much money will I get?"

"One hundred dollars," Dwayne told him. "That's four hundred dollars a month for you and Jeb."

Shorty took a thoughtful drink of coffee. He set the cup down. "What do you think, Jeb?"

"Count me in!"

"Then let's get them trucks a-rolling!"

Jeb laughed out loud and hollered to Katy. "Hey, woman! Get us some rye whiskey to salute the beginning of a fine business deal."

———

IT WAS AN EARLY SATURDAY EVENING WHEN Johnny Lewis drove from his duplex into the warehouse district of downtown Wichita. He slowed a bit, when he saw Maybelle standing on the sidewalk, waving to him. He pulled up to the curb giving her a big smile.

The girl walked over and got in the car. "Hi, Johnny. I was glad you called me to say you was coming."

"Why, sure!" he said. "You didn't think I'd stand you up, do you?"

"No. You're too nice of a boy to do anything mean."

He stepped on the accelerator and turned south to get to Kellogg street. "I think you're gonna like Mexican food.

My folks and me went to the El Charro a lot. But let me warn you. Some of their salsa is really, really hot. I like it, but I'll point out the sweet salsa for you."

"What's them salsas for, Johnny?"

"Salsa is sauce in Spanish. You can dip your food in it."

They arrived in the parking lot of El Charro Café and Johnny had no trouble finding a parking place. "This place will be packed in another hour," he said. "Then again late at night."

They entered the building and went to the rostrum of the maître d'. The gentleman gave them a table in the corner of the dining room. A friendly, smiling waiter appeared with menus, asking, "What can I get you for drinks?"

"Make it ice tea for both of us," Johnny said. He looked at Maybelle. "I think I'd better do the ordering since you don't know a lot about Mexican food. This café's got combination plates that are really good."

When the waiter returned with the drinks, he took out his notebook. "Okay, folks. What's your choices?"

Johnny asked for combination dinner 3 which was made up of an enchilada and tamale with frijole beans and Spanish rice. This was for Maybelle. He chose carne asada, frijole beans, and Spanish rice for himself. He also asked for both hot and sweet salsa. A few minutes later a bus boy showed up with a bowl of tortilla chips and two flavors of salsas.

Johnny picked up a chip and dipped into one of the small bowls. He took a bite and pointed to the other bowl. "That's the sweet salsa."

She followed his suggestion "Mmm! That's delicious!"

"I told you."

The waiter arrived with the main courses. "D'you want anything else?"

"Nope," Johnny answered.

Maybelle looked around the dining room at the Mexican décor. "This is a right pretty place."

"I've always liked it."

After they began eating, Maybelle praised the food that she had never experienced. She also became curious about the hot salsa and asked Johnny to put a small dab on her tamale.

"Are you sure?" he asked.

"I'd like to taste it."

Johnny put a drop on her tamale. Maybelle took one bite and her tongue felt like it was on fire as her eyes watered. She reached for her glass of ice tea and swallowed all of it in three gulps.

"I told you it was hot, didn't I?" Johnny asked with a grin.

"I have...never...had something...so hot...hot in my mouth!"

"It'll cool down quick enough," Johnny said. He checked his watch. "We've got enough time for desert before the movie starts."

"Whew! I'll take ice tea for dessert, if'n you don't mind, Johnny."

"I think you would be better off with *helado*. That's what they call ice cream here."

Johnny signaled to the waiter.

———

WHEN JOHNNY AND MAYBELLE ARRIVED AT THE theater, the young couple bought cokes and popcorn in the lobby, then went up to the balcony where smoking was allowed. Smooching was also ignored.

The lights dimmed to darkness and the program started with a newsreel. This was followed by a cartoon and a *Pete Smith* short subject. Next came the action-packed western, *Gunfighter* with Randolph Scott.

Johnny liked the shoot-outs while Maybelle was taken in by the romantic side of the movie. Maybelle wondered if Johnny would want to smooch. She was disappointed when he acted the perfect gentleman and didn't as much as hold hands with her.

After the showing, they went back to his car. "I got a good idea," he said. "Let's go to Armstrong's Ice Cream Parlor."

"Ain't that place across the street from the high school?"

"Yep. East High. That's where I went, but I got a hankering for the army and didn't take in my senior year."

When they reached the popular ice cream parlor it was crowded as to be expected on a Saturday night. They found a table in a rear corner and Johnny signaled to get the attention of a waitress. She hurried over and stood ready to take their order.

"I'll have a banana split," Johnny said. "What d'you want, Maybelle?"

"What's a banana split?"

The waitress broke in. "It's split a banana with three scoops of different flavors of ice cream on it. Then chocolate syrup and whipped cream are put on top of that. It's really good, hon."

"Okay," Maybelle said. "I'll take that split banana, too."

The order was prepared in the timely Armstrong way.

Maybelle could hardly believe her eyes. "I don't think I can eat this much, Johnny."

"Well, eat all you can, and I'll finish the rest."

The couple started in on the splits. After they had made some inroads into the delicious dishes, Johnny said, "Would you like to see where I live? It's a duplex uptown on Victor Street just east of Hillside."

"I'd love to, Johnny."

Fifteen minutes later Johnny had eaten all his banana split but Maybelle had hardly finished a quarter of hers. She sighed and pushed it over to him. "It's yours! I don't see how you can finish it though."

"Oh, yeah," Johnny said with a chuckle. "Watch this."

It took him ten minutes to eat it all and when finished he displayed a smile of contentment. "Ah! Now can we make a tour of my castle?"

After leaving the parking lot, Johnny drove farther east and reached Hillside. Maybelle wondered what would happen when they went inside his house. She began feeling unsure of herself.

Johnny pointed at another movie theater down the street. "That's the Uptown. They show pretty good movies. It's within walking distance of my place."

He went north a block then turned east to a residential neighborhood. After parking, he indicated a duplex on the corner. "That one on the left is mine."

They left the car and went up to the door. Johnny unlocked it and stepped back to let Maybelle enter. He followed her in and turned a light switch on by the door. "It's a pretty mess, ain't it?"

"No, Johnny," Maybelle said a bit nervously. "It's nice and it ain't cluttered too much."

"C'mon, I'll give you a tour." He took her across the front room into the kitchen. "It's pretty small but there's a stove and refrigerator that are in good shape." Next he showed her a bedroom. "The people that lived here before me left a cot. I ain't sure if I'm gonna keep it though."

He took her by the hand and led her to the next door. "This is my bedroom."

Maybelle liked the feel of his gentle grip. "So this is where you sleep, huh?"

Johnny turned and embraced her tenderly, looking into her eyes. "I want you, Maybelle." He regretted being so sudden. "I'm sorry."

Now Maybelle felt no discomfort as joyful ardor began settling into her psyche. "I want you, too, Johnny."

They walked up to the bed and began disrobing. The light from the living room gave a weak illumination that cast a shadow across their nakedness. Maybelle got on the bed and turned toward him. He reached in the bedstand drawer and pulled out a prophylactic packet.

The beautiful girl and handsome boy made love tenderly as a gentle passion built up between them. True love drifted over the couple with each kiss and caress.

———

IF THERE WAS EVER A CONTEST ON THE SPEED OF a man and woman falling into heartfelt love, the record champions would be Johnny Lewis and Maybelle Gilhooly. She spent the night and they enjoyed sexual exercise a total of three times. Between the lovemaking, they drank some beer Johnny had in the refrigerator and made small but romantic conversation.

They slipped into slumber at four o'clock in the morning.

———

AFTER THE COUPLE GOT UP AT MID-MORNING, they knew they loved one another and that wonderful night was the start of the rest of their lives together. They dressed languidly and Johnny suggested they go to his favorite café at Central Avenue and Hillside Street. It was a small, cozy eatery called *Billy Joe's Café*. They sat on the same side of the booth and ordered the pancake special.

"You know quite a bit about me," Johnny said. "So now it's my turn to learn about you."

Maybelle knew better than to be too truthful, so she skipped some horrible moments of hell she had endured. "Well, I lived in a house out in the country until not too long ago. It was south of Hutchinson but it wasn't on a farm. It just sits out there all by itself. I lived with my mother and three brothers."

"Was your dad living there, too?"

"He deserted us a long time ago. Anyhow, things had never been very nice. We was always short on cash money. So I decided to get away and I caught a bus to Wichita where I found the Randall Hotel. I was worried about not having enough money to stay there for very long but the lady that runs the place told me I could go across the street to the Salvation Army. They gave me some money to stay at the Randall then got me the job at the laundry and I ended up earning enough to stay. I got a roommate though. Her name is Sally Duncan. She works at the laundry, too."

"And here I am at that same laundry," Johnny said with a chuckle. "How about that." Then he added, "I'm sorry you had all that trouble, but if you hadn't gone through it we would never have met."

"I did have one good thing in that rundown house and that was my youngest brother Horatio. He was always nice and we really liked each other. The older brothers did

CHAPTER 23

Dwayne gave notice to Shorty and Jeb that he was going to leave Sunday morning. The shamus told them he had gotten a call at the motor court to check in with his gang leader. They had to arrange the first transport of the cigarettes from Oklahoma into Kansas.

"How long is 'at gonna take you, Dwayne?" Jeb asked.

"I'll be back Monday. My boss is gonna travel from New Orleans to meet me in Wichita to approve the arrangements I had made with Shorty and you. We can't talk about that stuff over the telephone or in writing. That way there won't be no slip-ups or problems to pass through to the Canadian border."

Shorty was impressed by being in a high-class outfit with plenty of money. "We'll be waiting for you, Dwayne."

Dwayne's real purpose of leaving was to go to Wichita to see Donna Sue and make sure she was alright. Then he'd call on Harry Philbin in the City Building office to bring him up to date on his investigation.

odd jobs around the county. I hated to leave Horatio, but I had to." She paused. "Let's see...he'd be about eighteen now."

Johnny spoke up. "Hey, Maybelle. Why don't we go up there to Hutchinson and get Horatio? If he's still living there, we could bring him back here to Wichita. He could sleep in that empty room on the cot until he got a job."

"Would you do that, Johnny?"

"Sure. Hutchinson ain't too far away. We could go up there next Sunday."

Tears came to her eyes. "You don't know how much that means to me, Johnny."

"If it makes you happy then it makes me happy."

———

JOHNNY AND MAYBELLE LEFT WICHITA SUNDAY morning to start up U.S. Highway 81 for their trip to get her brother Horatio. The girl was a bit worried. "I don't know what my ma is gonna say when we show up."

"Well, we can turn back any time you want, honey."

Maybelle sighed. "Let's keep going. I want to get Horatio away from her and them two older brothers of mine."

When they reached the town of Newton, Johnny turned west on U.S. 50, heading for Hutchinson. The young couple said nothing as they traveled until Maybelle spoke up. "Make a left at this next road, sweetie."

Once more, Johnny followed her instructions. Finally, she announced, "Take this turn-off." This led them on a narrow dirt road. Ten minutes later they could see a dilapidated old farmhouse. "That's it!"

Johnny eased off the road and crossed the open area in front of the tumble-down dwelling. He came to a stop close to the porch. He looked at her. "I reckon we're here."

Maybelle took a deep breath. "Let's get this over with, Johnny."

"Sure!" he said, trying to appear nonchalant.

They got out of the car and walked up on the porch. Maybelle opened the front door and walked into the interior. She called out, "Ma!"

Lilly Gilhooly made a quick appearance from the kitchen. Her eyes opened wide at the sight of her daughter. "It's you!" She turned her eyes on Johnny. "Who's he?"

"He's my sweetheart, Ma."

"Well, he's a hell of a lot better looking than that jasper you run away with."

Maybelle's face turned red and she wanted to change the subject. "I never stayed with him. As soon as we got to Wichita, I dumped him. I got a job in a laundry, Ma. This here's Johnny Lewis and he works there, too."

Lilly grinned. "Are you a washerman?"

Maybelle muttered, "He drives a delivery truck!"

Lilly shrugged. "That don't mean nothing to me. Anyhow, what'd you come back here for?"

"We...me and Johnny...have come to get Horatio. We aim to take him to Wichita where he can live in Johnny's house. And we're gonna get him a job, too."

Lilly looked stunned. Maybelle thought she was going to lose her temper, but the woman exclaimed, "Lord above! That's fine with me!"

Maybelle was surprised. "You mean that?"

"You bet I do, honey," she said in a happy tone of voice. "I want to get him away from Junior and Cornelius."

"Is Horatio with 'em now?"

"Nope. He's out back hoeing in the vegetable garden."

Maybelle took Johnny's hand and walked through the kitchen and out the back door. She called out, "Horatio!"

He looked up at her and let out a happy yell. "Maybelle! Oh, Maybelle! You've come back!"

She walked over to him and they hugged and held the embrace for a full minute with tears flowing. She pointed to Johnny. "We came to take you to Wichita. Me and him want you to leave here. You can live in Johnny's house and get a job."

Horatio walked over and offered his hand to Johnny. "I'm pleased to make your acquaintance."

Johnny nodded. "Likewise."

"Is that all right with Ma?" Horatio asked.

"That's the best part," Maribelle said. "She's happy for you to get the hell out here."

Lilly came outside. "Horatio, you go upstairs and get all your stuff. There's some boxes up there you can put ever'thing in. And do it now! I don't want you to be here when Junior and Cornelius come back. Especial Cornelius."

"You bet, Ma!" Horatio said, hurrying into the house.

———

DWAYNE DROVE ACROSS THE WICHITA CITY limits and went directly to his and Donna Sue's apartment. When he walked in, he found her doing a crossword puzzle in the *Wichita Eagle*. "Thank God!" She gave him a kiss on the mouth, another one on his cheek and one more on the mouth. "So! How're things going?"

"Do you remember that midnight reconnaissance we made? Well, now I've seen the place in the blaze of sunlight."

"How did you do that?"

"I made friends with a guy who not only works there but lives on the place along with his wife." He chuckled. "Y'know that steak you gave me for dogs? Well, the very one I gave it to came running up to me wagging his tail. I guess he was expecting some more meat."

"Oh, dear," Donna Sue said. "Poor little puppy."

"Anyhow, I pretty much got the run of the place. I can hang out there until those burglars show up with their loot."

"That sounds dangerous, Dwayne! You'll be right in

the middle of a whole group of bad men. I hate to think what they'd do to you if they find out you're a lawman."

"What I'm gonna do is call Harry Philbin. He can get a small posse together, and we'll go down there and start doing some enforcement of the law."

Donna Sue was worried about Dwayne's nerves over Tommy's murder. "You're not going to kill anyone, are you?"

"Naw," he said. "D'you want to go to the Continental Grill to eat?"

"Sure!"

"Then after supper we can go home and fool around, okay? I gotta leave in the morning."

Donna Sue smiled at him, but wasn't exactly thrilled.

CHAPTER 24

I t was Monday noon when Dwayne drove across the
bridge and continued deeper into Shorty Barlow's
property. When he parked in front of the warehouse, he
noticed an ancient automobile nearby. He got out and
gave it a close study, recognizing it as a Model A Ford
from the late twenties.

He went inside and saw two men putting kitchenware
on the counter in front of Shorty. The fence looked over
at him. "Howdy, Dwayne. How'd things go with you?"

"It won't be long now," Dwayne said.

Shorty nodded toward the two men. "These is the
Gilhooly boys, Dwayne. Junior and Cornelius. Boys, this
is Dwayne Thompson. He's got me a good deal in a first
class operation."

Dwayne's instinctive detective-side kicked in hard.
The Sunday burglars were standing almost nose-to-nose
with him. He controlled his emotions and simply nodded.
"Hi, ya." He turned to Shorty. "Is Jeb around?"

"Yeah, he's over to the house."

Dwayne walked around the back of the warehouse.

He sighted Katy Clemens running clothes through the wringer on her washing machine. He waved at her. "I see you got something to do."

"Yeah," she replied. "Them Gilhooly boys brought in a bunch of clothes and some of 'em was in laundry bags. Shorty can't sell none of 'em unless they're clean."

Dwayne found Jeb on the front porch of the house sitting in a rocking chair drinking a bottle of Schlitz Beer. "Howdy, Dwayne."

"How's it going, Jeb?"

"Not bad. Want a beer? You can get one from the refrigerator. On second thought, get me one, too. No! Four instead so we can both have a couple."

"I'll be right back."

Dwayne walked into the kitchen and took four beers out of the fridge. He returned to the porch and sat down on the straight-back chair. "It's lucky you got a generator here or you'd have to drink this brew warm."

"You're right about that."

Dwayne took a sip from the bottle of beer. "I met the Gilhooly boys over in the warehouse. That Model A they got looks like it gets plenty of good treatment."

"They take good care of it."

"Do they live close around here?"

"Sure, not far at all," Jeb replied. "Just go out the opposite way you came in and turn left. Keep going straight and you'll see a broken down house on the left. That's where they live."

"How many Gilhooly's are there?"

"They's four of 'em. Ma Gilhooly, Junior Gilhooly, Cornelius Gilhooly and Horatio Gilhooly."

"Just one female there huh?'

Jeb took a swallow of beer. "There used to be a young girl, but she ran off with some guy."

The two fell into silence, and Dwayne now knew that Maybelle Gilhooly was that girl. He feigned a look at his watch. "Wow! I got to get back to the motor court and make a phone call. You can have that other bottle of beer."

"Okay, Dwayne! Get us a big load of them cigarettes."

———

DWAYNE WENT TO THE PUBLIC TELEPHONE booth just outside the door of the motor court's lobby. He put a nickel in the slot. An operator answered, "Number please."

"I'd like to place a collect call to Wichita. 3803."

"One moment, please."

Dwayne waited as the woman went through the routine of long distance. She asked Harry Philbin if he would accept the call and he concurred.

"Hi, Dwayne. What's cooking?"

"We're close to the end, Harry. I met the Sunday burglars. I've seen them selling their loot and have the exact directions to their house out here in the country."

"Terrific! How many are there?"

"There was two, but I know there's another one."

"Okay. I can pull two of our agents out of the narcotics cases for a short time. Where can we meet up with you?"

"The Happy Traveler Motor Court south of Hutchinson on State 96. You'll find me in Cottage Three."

———

ON MONDAY EVENING, MAYBELLE AND JOHNNY began reading the want-ads in the *Wichita Eagle* and

Wichita Beacon newspapers to find work for Horatio. There wasn't much to be found for an eighteen-year-old who had quit school after the sixth grade.

The boy asked, "Perhaps I should join the army like you did, Johnny."

"Sorry," the ex-G.I. said, "but the services will only take guys with at least ten years of schooling. Since there ain't a war on, they can be sorta picky, if you know what I mean."

Maybelle wasn't discouraged. "There's lots of jobs in Wichita so don't worry. We'll find something."

"Yeah," Johnny agreed. "So let's sleep on it, hey. We'll try again tomorrow evening. In the meantime, I'm hankering for some of them pancakes in *Billy Joe's Café*."

Maybelle decided to sleep over in Johnny's duplex since Horatio was using the cot in the spare room. One benefit of having Maybelle's younger brother was his talent in cooking. Lilly Gilhooly had taught Horatio a lot about kitchen chores until the boy was old enough to join the criminal activities with his brothers.

———

ON MONDAY MORNING, JOHNNY AND MAYBELLE arrived at Whitaker's Laundry to punch in fifteen minutes before seven o'clock. Maybelle hurried to the laundering room and found Sally Duncan already there.

"Thank God!" Sally exclaimed. "When you didn't come home last night I was afraid something bad had happened to you."

"I got some good news, Sally! I went with Johnny to pick up my youngest brother Horatio! He's gonna live with Johnny 'til he gets settled down here in Wichita."

"Oh, Maybelle! Is he cute?"

"Well...he is your age."

"You're gonna introduce him to me, ain't you?"

"O'course, silly!"

The workday started and the two young women labored at their station, loading the washing machines then taking out the wet clothes to the drying room.

When the morning break was sounded, they went to the lunchroom for coffee and donuts as provided by the management. The first person they saw was Johnny with a wide grin on his face.

"Hi, sweetie," Maybelle said. "Did you finish your morning runs?"

"I did more than that," he said. "C'mon!"

He led her to the company office and opened the door. "Go on inside."

She went through the door and saw Horatio. "What are you doing here?"

"I'm gonna be a janitor!"

Maybelle embraced him. "How did you manage to do that?"

"I didn't manage it. I was at Johnny's place and he came walking in and told me to go with him."

Johnny broke in. "I checked the bulletin board and saw a notice for an opening with the cleaning staff. I went in and told 'em about Horatio. They told me to bring him in for an interview after my next run."

"They said I was perfect for the job," Horatio said. "And I start tomorrow morning!"

"Yeah," Johnny said. "I got to start my early afternoon run, so I'll go by the house and drop him off."

"Oh!" Maybelle sobbed. "Ain't ever'thing just wonderful!

CHAPTER 25

The quartet of lawmen—Dwayne, Harry Philbin and two K.B.I. agents—were gathered in Dwayne's room at the Happy Traveler Motor Court. The agents, Kirk and Fremont, had been temporarily pulled off the narcotics cases to back up Dwayne and Philbin in the raid on the Sunday burglars. Although Philbin was higher in rank, he turned the command duties to Dwayne who knew the best way to deal with the arrests.

Philbin, however, had brought items of equipment to be used in the night raid. These were dark coveralls, high-powered flashlights, and black face paint. The lawmen had their own handcuffs, pistols, and blackjacks or saps.

"Okay," Dwayne said, beginning his briefing. "Philbin and I will be in my car and you two guys take the other one. I've observed the target. It's a two-floor frame house that's seen better days. There are no electric wiring or telephone lines attached so we'll be charging into darkness. Keep your pistols in your shooting hands and the flashlights in the other."

Fremont asked, "Did you get a chance to see the layout of the interior?"

"No," Dwayne said. "So you and Kirk go through the back door and wait for me and Harry to enter the front door. At that point, turn on your flashlights. If there's nobody on the bottom floor, we'll charge up the stairs. And that's gotta be done fast."

"How many bad guys are there?" Kirk inquired.

"I got word that there's three men and one old woman who is their mother."

Philbin laughed. "We got a Ma Barker, huh?"

"Good God I hope not!" Dwayne said.

"By the way," Philbin said. "I sent info on that fencing racket up to headquarters, and they're going to turn it over to the Highway Patrol. They'll hold off until we've got the Sunday crooks in custody."

"Well, guys," Dwayne said. "Let's settle down and do a bit of napping until 0400 hours."

————

DWAYNE, WITH PHILBIN SITTING AT HIS SIDE, turned off the headlights while approaching the house from the north. Fremont was driving with Kirk beside him and he followed suit. The night sky had a full moon. But that wouldn't bother the raid since the action would be in the house. The raiding team stopped the vehicles out in the dirt road. They resembled commandos with their coveralls and the black streaks on their faces. All had pistols and flashlights ready.

"Let's go!" Dwayne said.

Kirk and Fremont moved silently to the back of the house while Dwayne and Harry Philbin walked around the Model A Ford in the front. They gingerly stepped on the floorboards of the porch. There were no squeaks so they step-toed across to the door. Dwayne took hold of the doorknob. It opened silently as he pushed it inward. They both stepped inside and saw that Fremont and Kirk had turned on their flashlights where the kitchen was. Dwayne and Philbin did the same and lit up the combination parlor and dining room.

There were stairs on the east side, and Dwayne stepped carefully up to the second floor with the others following. The teams split up and checked out the bedrooms. Dwayne was disappointed. There was the snoring woman but two men not three. One of them was obviously missing.

"Leave the woman alone," Dwayne whispered. "And let's do this by teams." He nodded to Fremont and Kirk. "You two go to that far door. Me and Harry will take this one. Wait for my command."

A couple of beats followed then Dwayne yelled, "Hit 'em!"

They all charged in and grabbed the sleeping men, pulling them off their beds and onto the floor. The Gilhoolys were stunned when they were pulled to their feet and had their hands cuffed behind them. Lilly had slept through the takedown.

Dwayne and Harry had Junior. He panted and looked at his captors in the illumination of the flashlights. Their blackened faces shook him up badly. "Who in hell are you guys? What d'you want?"

Philbin answered him. "You're under arrest for armed burglary and murder."

"The hell if I am!"

Dwayne grabbed him by the scruff of the neck and smashed his face against the wall three times. Junior stumbled back and fell on the bed. The shamus pulled him to the floor and gave him three hard kicks in the ribs.

"Dwayne!" Philbin said. "Take it easy, okay?"

"One of these bastards killed my best friend!"

Philbin pulled Junior to his feet and led him out into the hall. Fremont and Kirk stood with Cornelius also wearing handcuffs. He glared at Dwayne and the shamus threw an uppercut that bounced the burglar off the wall. Blood spurted from his mouth. Dwayne turned to the team. "I'm gonna get the old bitch up."

The shamus went down to Lilly's bedroom and pulled her covers off. Then he grabbed her by the hair and pulled her off the bed. She ended up on the floor shrieking in pain. Now she noticed a strange man with a black streaked face was pulling her to stand up.

"Junior!" she screamed. "It's the devil hisself!"

Dwayne pushed her out into the hall and steered her over to her injured sons.

Lilly was astonished and terrified. "Who...what is...my boys...my boys–"

Dwayne announced, "I am arresting you for armed burglary and murder." He pulled her back into the bedroom. "Get dressed!"

The fact that a strange man was going to view her in the nude made things seem even more terrifying to the woman. Fremont and Kirk had ordered Junior and Cornelius to get dressed. In ten minutes the Gilhooly clan was being forced down the stairs and out to the vehicles.

―――――

AT THE SAME TIME OF THE RAID ON THE Gilhooly clan, a combined force of the K.B.I. and Kansas Highway Patrol carried out a raid on Shorty Barlow's compound in Reno County. Shorty, Jeb and Katy Clemens were taken into custody. Jeb wanted to cut a deal, telling the officers that he knew about a guy who sold untaxed cigarettes. He quickly had second thoughts when he realized the smugglers were probably a large gang and would send a hit man to take care of him for squealing.

A third incursion was conducted by the Highway Patrol and K.B.I. This was at the place known as Four Corners in Sumner County. George and Wanda Carson were arrested in their house. This was the couple that owned the filling station, garage and café. At first George denied doing anything illegal, but a Highway Patrol sergeant informed him the law was familiar with his chop shop operation. At that point George wouldn't identify his two employees who lived in Wellington. But he caved in when his wife Wanda pointed out there was really nothing to gain in the present situation.

"You just cooperate, George! We're in bad trouble! It'll be better for us clam up and get an attorney."

George Carson nodded his agreement.

———

DWAYNE AND HIS K.B.I. COMPANIONS DROVE TO Wichita with their prisoners. They didn't waste time in turning them over to the Sedgewick County Jail. Lilly Gilhooly was taken to the women's side while her two sons were put into separate cells. With that done, Harry Philbin sent Fremont and Kirk back on the narcotics beat.

When Dwayne and Philbin went outside to the jail-house parking lot, the shamus went to the K.B.I. car he had been using. He took off the license plates he'd gotten from Elmer Pettibone. He replaced them with the official

ones of the Kansas government since he was still assigned
to the K.B.I. Philbin knew Dwayne had wanted to make
the car look unofficial to cover his identity. But he
thought it better not to ask him where he got the plates.
The shamus' reputation for solving cases in unconven-
tional styles was well known in local law enforcement.

Dwayne dropped Philbin off at the City Building
then headed for his apartment.

Donna Sue was having breakfast when he came
through the door.

"What in the world is on your face?"

"I've been playing commando." He walked over to his
wife and planted a quick kiss on her forehead. "I got some
crazy news for you. The Sunday morning burglaries was
done by Maybelle's brothers. The mother was their
guiding light."

Donna Sue's eyes opened wider. "Really?"

"Yeah. There should have been three of 'em but only
two were available."

"Dwayne, listen. Maybelle and her boyfriend went up
to Reno County and brought the youngest brother back
here to Wichita this past week. His name is Horatio and
he's the youngest one."

"What was that all about?"

"I just found out about it yesterday. Maybelle told me
she wanted to get the young guy to Wichita. Her
boyfriend is letting the kid live with him since Maybelle
lives in that hotel. The three of 'em all work at the
Whitaker Laundry."

"I've got a warrant of armed burglary and murder for
Horatio Gilhooly!"

"I don't think he did it, Dwayne! I've met him and
he's an eighteen-year-old kid."

"There's a law in Kansas that if there is a murder

committed, everyone connected to the crime will be punished the same. I got the warrant and I'm gonna go to that laundry right now and serve it on him."

"Oh, Dwayne! Wash your face first!"

————

DWAYNE, WITH A CLEAN FACE, WALKED through the front door of the Whitaker Laundry. The man behind the counter came over to see what he wanted. "May I help you, sir?"

The shamus showed his K.B.I. badge. "I believe you've got an employee by the name of Horatio Gilhooly."

"I'm not sure," the man said with wide-open eyes. "I'll fetch somebody from the office." He walked over to an inner-connect telephone and pressed the button on it. "A policeman wants to find out about a—" He turned to look at Dwayne. "What is that employee's name again?"

"Horatio Gilhooly."

The man repeated the name and hung up. "One of our office staff is on their way."

A man well dressed in a suit and tie appeared. "Yes. We have a new employee on our janitorial staff by the name of Horatio Gilhooly. I can take you to him if you wish."

"Yeah. I wish."

Dwayne was escorted through the building to a hall-way. He saw a janitor swishing a mop on the floor. He recognized the resemblance of a Gilhooly. The shamus walked up behind him, and spun him around.

"I am arresting you for armed burglary and the murder of Thomas Brady."

CHAPTER 26

After the paperwork of jailing Horatio Gilhooly, it was early evening and Dwayne drove back to the apartment. Donna Sue heard his familiar key in the lock and hurried over to the kitchen counter to get him the Jack Daniels liquor he liked so well.

He grinned when she handed him the full glass. "Okay, babe. Let's go over and sit down on our favorite sofa so I can give you the latest."

"Wait 'til I get my chardonnay." She walked over to the kitchen counter and poured a glass. Then they settled down. "Now thrill me!"

Dwayne seemed to be in a very good mood. "We've got everything wrapped up with the arrests. The trial is the next thing."

"I suppose that's going to keep you busy."

"Yeah. By the way I arrested the young kid Horatio. He was working at the laundry as a janitor."

"Maybelle is going to be devastated. Horatio is her youngest brother. The two are very close."

Dwayne frowned. "That kid, like his fucking brothers, is going to be tried for murder in a court of law. That makes me very happy since the victim was the best friend I ever had."

"I know, Dwayne. You don't have to tell me again. But Maybelle must be going through hell." Donna Sue finished her wine. "Listen, sweetie. I want to go over to the hotel and see how she's doing. Okay?"

"Sure," Dwayne replied with a shrug.

Donna Sue got her sweater and purse. "I won't be long."

She hurried over to the parking garage to get the Nash station wagon. The drive over to the Randall Hotel was only ten minutes. Daisy Randall looked up as she walked into the lobby.

"Hello, Donna Sue. Maybelle came in here earlier and she was crying."

"I know," Donna Sue said. "She's having a hard time of it right now."

"It's probably none of my business, but I'd like to know about it."

"Those burglars in the news are her brothers."

Daisy gasped. "I read about that in the *Eagle*."

"It's all over Wichita," Donna Sue said. "See you later."

She went up the stairs and knocked on the door. Sally Duncan answered and stepped back to let her in. "Oh, Donna Sue! Maybelle was fired from the laundry."

Maybelle, who was sitting on her bed, got up and went over to embrace Donna Sue. "Dwayne arrested Horatio this afternoon. Why did he have to do that? And now I don't have a job. The boss told me I wasn't the sort they wanted to have as an employee. I'll have to leave the hotel."

Donna Sue held her close. "Dwayne and I can help you, honey."

Maybelle stepped back. "It's Dwayne's fault! Horatio is a nice boy!"

Donna Sue almost answered when there was another knock on the door. Sally opened it to see Johnny Lewis. He walked over to Maybelle and took her in his arms. "I heard what happened when I checked out."

"Oh, Johnny! What am I going to do?"

"You're moving in with me, honey."

"I was afraid you wouldn't want me no more."

"It was all your brothers' fault and you had nothing to do about it."

"Is it okay if I get my things and go with you right now?"

"That's why I'm here," Johnny told her. "I told the lady downstairs I came to get you. But we got to keep you pretty much out of sight, honey. Unmarried couples living together are against the law, y'know."

Donna Sue and Sally watched as Maybelle began packing her meager belonging.

———

THE NEXT DAY THE DISTRICT ATTORNEY'S Office announced that the trial of the Gilhooly brothers would be in Wichita. Although none of the felonies were committed in that city, there were too many separate counties to hold complete court proceedings in each. The prosecutor would be District Attorney Wyatt Cunningham while the defender would be Carl Banter, a local attorney.

Wichitans were surprised to read newspapers and hear radio news broadcasts about the thefts from country residences on Sunday mornings. To make it more interesting to the public, the murder of Tommy Brady in Butler Country was part of the crime wave. All this had been published in both the *Wichita Eagle* and the *Wichita Beacon* earlier in the week.

The *Wichita Eagle's* crime reporter Bobby Terwilliger, who wanted to get some more confidential information, called the Wheeler Detective Agency. Donna Sue answered the call and passed it over to Dwayne.

The shamus picked up his phone. "Hey, Bobby! I bet I know what you want."

"Yeah. I want some real info on this crazy criminal group."

"You're in luck," Dwayne said. "I've just about wrapped up most of the paperwork on the caper, but I'm still on call. So how about you coming over here?"

Dwayne hung up and Donna Sue, who had been listening sighed. "This whole thing is making me so very, very sad."

"I wish you'd remember that Tommy was murdered by that gang!"

"I'm thinking of Maybelle, honey. She didn't know what her brothers were up to until they were arrested."

Bobby Terwilliger showed up quickly after his phone call. He walked in and Donna Sue led him around the partition to Dwayne's desk. The reporter shook hands with the shamus.

"Have a seat, Bobby. Donna Sue is gonna take notes for our files. Is that okay?"

Terwilliger laughed. "Hell, yes! This is really gonna piss off the *Beacon*."

"You guys are really competitive, aren't you?" Dwayne said.

"You damn right we are," Terwilliger said. "Well, let's

get down to business. I want to start out about that gang of murdering burglars."

"Okay, here goes. The outfit was made up of an elderly lady and her three sons."

"Man!" the reporter said. "It's like Ma Barker and her boys all over again."

Donna Sue broke in. "Who's Ma Barker?"

"She was like Lilly Gilhooly," Terwilliger said. "She led her boys in a life of crime that ranged from robbery to murder. She and one of her sons were finally cornered and killed in January 1935 in Florida."

Donna Sue frowned. "That's an unholy family if there ever was one!"

The interview went on with Dwayne revealing his appointment in the Kansas Bureau of Investigation. Dwayne revealed Shorty Barlow's fencing operation and the information on every farmhouse that had been robbed.

Terwilliger happily scribbled the information in his notebook. He paused and asked for the lowdown on the Gilhooly clan.

"Sorry, Bobby," Dwayne said. "I can't discuss anything about those guys or any other witnesses or defendants."

"Understood, my friend," Terwilliger said, standing up. "I've got enough to get you a place in an *Eagle* Sunday extra." He stuck his notebook in his jacket pocket. "Thanks, Dwayne. You, too, Mrs. Wheeler."

The newspaperman left and Dwayne leaned back in his chair. "I can't wait to see what Bobby writes."

Donna Sue got to her feet. "I'm gonna type up my notes." She gave Dwayne a sad look. "I really hate all this."

CHAPTER 27

Dwayne was summoned to Harry Philbin's bailiwick the first thing the next morning. He drove over to the City Building in the K.B.I. Chevrolet Coupé. When he entered the lobby of the building, he found that the elevators were on the higher floors. The shamus was so impatient that he trotted across the lobby to the stairwell taking two steps at a time.

He walked in Philbin's door, breathing hard and asking, "What's up, Harry?"

"We've got orders for you and me to go out to the Gilhooly house to search for more clues. I'm going to take along my satchel of judicial papers in case of any legal problems. There's also been a report that the gang had made a purchase of a car at Timmons Used Cars in Hutchinson."

"Really? I knew about the Model A Ford. This is the first time I've heard of another car."

"I don't know any more about it than you do," Philbin said. "We'll check out the burglars' residence first."

"There wasn't much to find in that place, as I remember."

"D'you have your car downstairs?" Philbin asked.

"It's ready and waiting."

———

THE TRIP UP TO THE GILHOOLY DOMAIN WAS A quiet one for the two lawmen. The pair didn't talk much as they headed up Kansas State Highway 96. They were numb from investigations, reports and other paperwork. Philbin stretched and yawned.

"I'll sure be glad when this is all over with."

"That District Attorney Cunningham is getting on my nerves," Dwayne said.

"He's kind of uppity," Philbin admitted. "More than once I had to remind him I'm in the K.B.I. not the District Attorney's office."

Dwayne tossed a cigarette out of the driver's side window. "I've been thinking about going on another vacation with Donna Sue after all this is done. Just a quick three or four days."

"Sure. That'll freshen you up."

Dwayne turned off the state highway onto country roads. A half an hour later they saw the Model A sitting undisturbed in the yard of the Gilhooly house. Dwayne pulled in and parked by the jalopy. When the duo walked up on the porch they saw the door was closed, indicating no one had kicked it in. Their entry into the house gave them another surprise. The interior was untouched.

"I guess farm folks around here ain't much on looting," Dwayne said.

"That makes it easier for us. Let's start combing the ground floor."

The two lawmen didn't have much to find in the front room of the house. There was some threadbare furniture including a sofa. They flipped it over to check out the bottom.

"Nothing here," Dwayne remarked.

The next stop was the kitchen. It was cluttered, but in a weird sort of order. After crawling, pulling and pushing through the cabinets, there were no items of interest.

"The Gilhoolys certainly didn't have very much," Philbin stated.

"C'mon," Dwayne said. "Maybe we'll have better luck upstairs."

The first bedroom was completely empty. "This must be where the kid Horatio slept," Dwayne surmised.

"It's downright barren," Philbin observed.

Next was Lilly's room. The first time they were there, they had pulled everything out of the dresser drawers and found a stash of greenbacks and coins. The next place was Cornelius' messy abode.

"Waste of time," Philbin remarked. They went into Junior's room. "Let's check out this habitat."

"It's another dead end," Dwayne said after looking around. "Just the bed we kicked over and that wooden stool in the corner."

"When you're right, you're right, ol' buddy."

They took a couple of steps toward the door just as Dwayne glanced up at the rafters. "Wait! I see something." He got the stool, and stepped up on it to see exactly what it might be. "There's a tin box here."

Philbin chuckled. "That's prob'ly where he kept his chewing tobacco."

Dwayne stepped down, and opened the box. "Holy shit, this is money!"

"Let me see," Philbin said. He reached in and pulled

out the cash. "Mmm, most of it's bound in paper strips, but there's some loose bills, too."

"Wait a minute!" Dwayne stated. "One of the farmers, a rich guy by the name of Tom Shaw, said he had thirty thousand dollars stolen."

Philbin laboriously counted the wrapped-up bundles. After ten minutes he announced, "Each of these packets have twenty dollars. Let's see 450 packets of twenty dollar bundles makes...nine thousand dollars."

"And some loose bills," Dwayne said. "Wait a minute. There should have been more. That farmer said the burglars took thirty thousand dollars of his money."

"Well," Philbin said, "those thieves prob'ly squandered the dough like drunken sailors."

"We better hurry and check in with that used car salesman," Dwayne said. "Be careful with the tin box."

"Not to worry, pal. I'll carry it like it's filled with diamonds."

They returned to the car and went back to the highway leading into Hutchinson. Philbin had the directions to the car lot. "It's on the other side of town. Just stay on Fifth Avenue. Our destination is just past Halstead Street."

Dwayne drove down the avenue for a few minutes, then Philbin said, "There it is. Timmons Used Cars." He slipped the tin box under the seat, but kept his satchel with him.

Dwayne drove up to the small building serving as an office. Timmons had spotted them approaching. He stepped out as the two lawmen climbed out of their car. "Hello, gentlemen. What can I do for you?" He looked with nervous curiosity at Philbin's satchel.

Both Dwayne and Philbin showed their K.B.I. badges.

Philbin said, "We have some questions, if you don't mind."

"Ask away, gents."

Philbin said, "We've been informed that you sold a 1941 Oldsmobile to a couple of guys named Gilhooly."

"I sold a 1941 Oldsmobile to two fellers named Smith," Timmons said. "I remember 'em for two reasons. Those guys paid me in cash money and they drove in here in a Model A Ford."

"That's them, all right. Did they give you any information as to where they were gonna drive that Oldsmobile?"

"They sure did and it wasn't far," Timmons said. "They drove it directly into my garage to be parked over there. The front is the repair shop where we prepare cars for selling. I also keep rented cars there for storage. C'mon, I'll show you."

"Just a minute," Dwayne said. "D'you have the keys."

"Sure do," Timmons said. "I keep the keys of all the rentals." He went into the office and came out with an ignition key and a trunk key. He handed them to Dwayne then led them over to a barn-like building. There were two mechanics working on an old Studebaker in the repair shop. Several automobiles were covered by tarpaulins. Timmons walked up to one and pulled the covering off.

"This is it."

Dwayne pointed to the lift in the front of the building. "We're going to need to inspect the underside of the car. Is it okay if we use your lift?"

"No problem," Timmons said. He gestured to one of the mechanics. "Fred, drive this Olds over to the lift. Get it up high enough so they can stand under it."

The mechanic wordlessly performed the request, then went back up to the front of the building. Philbin pulled a flashlight out of his satchel, making Dwayne laugh. "What else have you got in that valise of yours?"

"Well, there isn't any liquor, so you wouldn't be interested."

Philbin shined the light around the bottom of the car, checking out the driveshaft, muffler, differential and other places beneath it.

Timmons said. "You ain't gonna find anything since them boys never came back to drive the vehicle off the lot."

"We appreciate the info," Philbin said. "But we're not taking chances on anything."

Dwayne went over to the lever of the lift and pushed it down to lower the car. He drove it back to the rental side of the garage. The two lawmen began searching the auto. They took out the seats and looked carefully into every corner. Then the lawmen turned their attention to the trunk and beneath the hood.

Dwayne looked at him. "Nothing."

"I told you," Timmons said.

Philbin took a form out of his satchel and put it on the hood. "I'm gonna make out a report that will show this car is the property of the State of Kansas. You'll get a carbon copy. So we'll be keeping those keys. The Kansas Bureau of Investigation will send someone out to pick it up. Understood?"

"Yes, sir," Timmons said. "I hope they put the seats back in."

"Not to worry," Philbin said.

With that done, Dwayne and Philbin went back to the K.B.I. car to return to Wichita.

CHAPTER 28

District Attorney Wyatt Cunningham and Attorney Carl Banter walked into the outer office of Judge William Dodge. They were greeted by the judge's receptionist. She pressed down on the intercom and announced, "Mister Wyatt and Mister Banter have arrived, Your Honor...yes, sir." She looked up at the visitors. "His Honor said for you to go on in."

The judge, sitting at his desk, gave them a grin of welcome. "Sit down, gentleman and let's get things settled for the trial of those Gilhooly yokels." He watched as they pulled papers from their satchels.

Judge Dodge started with, "The first thing I want to let you know is that Lilly Gilhooly will not be tried by me. She's being kept isolated from those sons of hers. The lady —and I use that word recklessly—will be tried by Judge Eddie Watson."

"I was expecting that," Cunningham said.

The judge continued. "To save the State of Kansas money, we will try the three boys all at once." He picked up a paper from his desk. "The malefactors are Timothy

Junior twenty-four years of age; Cornelius twenty-two years of age; and Horatio eighteen years of age. Any questions or statements?"

"Yes, Bill," Banter said. "I'd like to discuss the youngest of the brothers. That, of course, would be Horatio. I have had several conversations with the boys' sister. Her name is Maybelle Gilhooly and she has given me some information on Horatio."

"Fire away, Carl."

"She informed me that Horatio Gilhooly has been under the influence and domination of his mother and older brothers all his life. The woman pulled him out of school as soon as he finished the eighth grade."

Cunningham interjected, "That's the maximum amount of education under Kansas state law. That and morons who are too stupid to get to the eighth grade. They can leave school when they reach the age of sixteen."

"That's true," Banter conceded, "but Miss Gilhooly told me that Horatio had been an excellent student and did not want to end his education. Mrs. Gilhooly would not give in to his begging to stay in school. She did this to dominate all three boys so that they could be a money team by breaking and entering, shoplifting, pilfering and other ways of lawlessness."

Judge Dodge raised a hand to break into Banter's spiel. "Hold it, please, Carl. I know what you're leading up to. And that would be to give the kid a break. Well, that isn't gonna happen. The three boys broke into a farmhouse in Butler County and were surprised when the owner suddenly appeared. One of them shot and killed the man. The law says that any crime committed that results in murder means all participating in the felony will be punished for the killing."

"The kid is eighteen-years-old," Cunningham said. "That means he's an adult in this state."

"Very true," Banter said. "But surely, if he was unable to escape from his evil family's dominance at such a young age, he could plead for mercy."

Cunningham frowned. "He'll have to do that *after* he has been sentenced and is confined to the penitentiary in Lansing. If he does, I'll lower the boom on him but good."

"All right," the Judge stated. "Let's continue with the protocol we'll be observing."

The three men of law began a lengthy discussion that went on into the afternoon.

DWAYNE SENSED SOME TENSION IN DONNA SUE after his return to Wichita. They had gone to the Stockyards Restaurant for steak dinners and she barely spoke during the meal. This made him a bit on edge, thinking he might have done something that irritated her. If so, he would be exposed to a lengthy reprimand sometime in the near future.

Donna Sue was the same after they finished eating and went back to their apartment. When they were inside he braced himself for a dressing down, but she was still somber and quiet. The couple followed their usual practice of treating themselves to Jack Daniels and chardonnay. She brought the drinks to the sofa and sat down.

"Dwayne, I have something to tell you. And I know you're probably going to be angry."

Now Dwayne knew it was something that *she* had done. He breathed a sigh of relief. "I'm sure it couldn't be too serious."

"Maybelle and I have an appointment with Carl Banter that involves her brother Horatio."

Now Dwayne was suspicious. "Yeah? What about that little bastard?"

"Since Carl is the lawyer for the Gilhooly brothers, we are going to see if Horatio can get a much lighter sentence than the others."

Dwayne's eyes widened and his face reddened with anger. "I'll be goddamned if you will!"

"You're not going to stop us, Dwayne!" she stated firmly. "So you might just as well get used to it."

"Don't you care that he was involved in Tommy's murder?"

"You know how I feel about his death," Donna Sue said. She was angered by his question and gave him one of her ferocious glares. "And I'm gonna tell you something else! I'm hiring Maybelle to be my assistant in the office."

Dwayne's jaw dropped. "What? Why?"

"She lost her job at the laundry and I want her to be as respectable as possible to the public." Donna Sue finished her wine, then took the glass back to the kitchen. "I've said all that I'm going to, Dwayne."

That was one of her moods that always drove her husband into silence. He watched her go over into the bedroom.

"There's gonna be a hot time in the old town for quite a while."

———

DONNA SUE WHEELER AND MAYBELLE GILHOOLY entered the Central Building in downtown Wichita and headed up to the fifth floor. When the two women reached the door of Carl Banter's outer office, they walked in.

The lawyer's secretary Judy Miller looked up with a smile. "Right on time." She turned to the intercom and pressed on the button. "Carl, your ten o'clock has arrived."

Banter appeared in the door of his office. "Hello, ladies! I'm very excited by your visit. Please come in." He looked over at his secretary. "You may follow, Judy. Be sure you bring your steno book."

After the women had settled down in chairs around Banter's desk, he said. "The telephone call from Mrs. Wheeler intrigued me. I have only a slight knowledge of Horatio Gilhooly and sought to get him a break. However, both Judge Dodge and D.A. Cunningham were adamant in their refusal for such an action." He paused and nodded to Mrs. Wheeler and Miss Gilhooly. "Which of you ladies wish to speak first?"

Donna Sue spoke up. "I told Miss Gilhooly that she should begin describing the unhappiness that Horatio had in the company of his mother and brothers. He has no knowledge whatsoever of his father." She turned to Maybelle. "You can speak now."

Maybelle's voice had a slight tremor when she started with a description of a house with no electricity or running water. There was an outdoor privy, and all the broken windows had been patched with plywood.

"Mmm," Banter murmured. "Was there much sickness because of this?"

"Yes, sir," Maybelle said. "Winter always brought up coughing and fevers. When Ma had the money, she bought Vicks for that. When one of us was hurt she had iodine and band-aids. We never went to a doctor a'tall."

"I see," Banter said. "Now tell me about Horatio."

"Yes, sir. He was the youngest of the boys and the smartest. He liked going to school and got good marks. The principal of the school came over to the house one time and talked to Ma about how smart he was, but Ma didn't give it no mind. In fact, she pulled Horatio out of school when he finished the eighth grade. I remember how sad it was for him. He cried for a long time. He liked to read his schoolbooks, but they was took away from him when he didn't come back to the ninth grade."

"How was his relationship with his brothers, Maybelle?"

"They was always teasing and making fun of him. Sometimes they hit him when he had done something they didn't like."

Maybelle took another fifteen minutes to answer questions from Banter with Judy taking down every word in her expert shorthand.

"All right, ladies," Banter said. "You can rest assured that I am going to look into this. It is possible to get some sympathy from the jury, but trials can be strange in their verdicts."

CHAPTER 29

Timothy Gilhooly A.K.A Junior sat across the table in the Sedgewick County Jail's consultation room. He was facing Attorney Carl Banter.

The lawyer leaned forward. "I'm here to discuss your youngest brother."

"Okay," Junior said. "But I ain't seen him a'tall since they keep him away from me and Cornelius."

"There is a chance that I can get him a much shorter sentence than you two fellows."

Junior crossed his arms over his chest. "That's inter'st-ing." In truth, he was extremely happy that his youngest brother could be getting a break. He was ready to help Horatio. He knew that somehow the youngest brother had to be separated from him and Cornelius.

"What do you and Cornelius think of Horatio?" Banter inquired.

Junior took a deep breath. "Me and Cornelius ain't much fond of him. We only took him on the burglaries to help carry extra stuff. We was always mean to him. I guess he thought he was smarter 'cause he did a lot better'n me and Cornelius in school. It'd make me and Cornelius pissed off when he acted uppity. When he done that we'd give him a smack across the chops."

"Did you hit him hard?"

"Hell! We kicked him lots of times and yelled at him 'cause he didn't like to work on our Model A car with us. When we was really mad, we'd make him drop his pants and we'd beat his ass with our leather belts 'til it was black and blue."

"I see," Banter remarked. "Would you and Cornelius be willing to testify as to the way you inflicted pain and fear on Horatio?"

"Sure. What the hell? Me and Cornelius are looking on being in jail 'til the day we die. The ain't no sense for Horatio to be with us."

"Okay," Banter said. A plan leaped quickly into his mind when he remembered what Maybelle had said. "I'm going to draw up some depositions on what you just told me. Then I'll bring them back here for you and Cornelius to sign."

Junior watched the lawyer leave the room, then got up to be escorted back to the cell he shared with Cornelius. When he was locked in, he motioned for his brother to come closer.

"Whatta you have, Junior?" Cornelius asked.

"I just got Horatio a break. He won't have to stay long in the pokey."

"Goddamn! That's just great, ain't it?" He paused. "How're we gonna do that, Junior?"

"I told our lawyer that we was always beating on him and being mean to him and making him drop his drawers and spanking his ass with our belts."

"But we never done any of that, Junior."

"O'course we never done any of that! But the law is

gonna think we did them things to make him go with us on them Sunday mornings."

Cornelius turned that information over in his mind, then caught on. "Junior, you're a good brother."

"Yeah!" Junior said. "Ma will be proud of us."

———————

TWO DAYS LATER, CARL BANTER WAS IN JUDGE Dodge's chamber, watching the Judge and District Attorney Wyatt Cunningham carefully perusing the depositions he had written. The paperwork was signed by Junior and Cornelius Gilhooly and concerned Horatio Gilhooly.

Banter had taken Judy Miller's typing of shorthand notes, and stuck in a heavy dose of legalism and other text. This was what the Judge and Cunningham now browsed through.

It took them a half hour to digest the whole thing. Cunningham laid his copy of the deposition aside. "I'm against it. The little bastard is from a criminal family and will eventually break the law again whether he's been mistreated or not. It's in his blood."

The Judge was thoughtful for a few moments. "I think you're wrong, Wyatt. This kid was helpless in the environment he lived in."

Cunningham disagreed. "If he gets an early release from jail he'll just go back to crime on the streets. He and his big brothers are going to spend the rest of their lives in confinement. If we could charge them with first degree murder, they would all be hanged. But that's not going to happen...unfortunately."

Banter spoke up. "Horatio was pulled out of school after he finished the eighth grade, Wyatt. The boy made high grades and when he was taken away from getting an education, he wept. He *wept*! Right now he's kept separate from his older brothers."

The Judge looked at Carl Banter. "I want you to write up a request to transfer the youngster to the jail clinic in Saint Michael Hospital for a psychiatric examination. Get it back to me as fast as possible."

Banter put his paperwork back in his satchel. "As they say in the army, Judge. I'll do it immediately if not sooner!"

Carl Banter hurried from the courthouse to drive to the Sedgewick County Jail. Upon arriving, he checked in and requested the presence of Horatio Gilhooly in the consultation room. He then went to the location and waited.

Fifteen minutes later Horatio appeared under escort by a jail guard who left him with his attorney. Banter shook the kid's hand as he sat down. "Horatio, I have some good news for you."

"Is that right, Mister Banter?"

"You may have suffered physical cruelty and harassment from your brothers, but that mistreatment is going to be in your favor now."

Horatio shrugged. "I never suffered anything that bad. I was teased a little bit, but that's all."

Banter felt like he had been slapped across the face. "Your brother Junior told me your life was a living hell! He said you were constantly bullied and beaten with leather belts!"

"That is not so, sir."

The attorney was puzzled for a few seconds then realized that Junior made up the cruelty and bullying so Horatio could get a break. "Horatio, my lad, you have brothers who love you."

Horatio was confused for a moment then declared, "They must've said I was beaten up so I could get a lesser sentence."

"That is correct, Horatio," Banter said. "What we have to do now, is make it look like your life was a miserable existence. And you can also say that your mother pulled you out of school and you cried about it."

"That was true, Mister Banter. I loved school and I was getting good grades, too. Ma needed me to help Junior and Cornelius."

"Better yet! Judge Dodge wants me to request a transfer for you to go to the Saint Michael Hospital jail clinic. You'll be going there for a psychiatric examination."

Horatio grinned. "This is going to be quite amusing. I shall make it look like I'm as crazy as a loon."

"Not quite, Horatio. You make it look like you're a miserable teenager who was cruelly treated. Not insane. And play up your expulsion from school, too."

"Yes, sir. I can easily do that."

"Okay, I'll send in requests to Judge Dodge for you to be moved to the hospital."

———

DOCTOR DURWARD CRAWFORD WAS AN excellent and respected psychiatrist with a good practice in Wichita, Kansas. He earned a bountiful amount of money from well-to-do patients who needed his professional help. However, there was always a small number of wealthy people who visited him simply looking for attention. They were the ones he would charge the most money.

Doctor Crawford was absent from his office after

being called into the Army during the war. He was stationed at various military hospitals treating soldiers who had been in battle and suffered from combat fatigue. These were a great challenge to his professional skill, and when he helped a patient back to health it gave him a deep feeling of personal self-gratification.

When he returned to civilian life in Wichita, the doctor reorganized his practice and once again began earning good money. After a year he had built an excellent reputation for his skills in helping people suffering from emotional disorders. Anytime silly malingerers appeared, he played games with their phony therapy.

When the Wichita chief of police heard of Doctor Crawford, he went to his office to see if the doctor would be willing to work in the jail clinic in Saint Michael Hospital.

"It won't pay much, Doctor," the Chief said. "You'll have irregular hours on a part-time schedule. And the pay will be much smaller that you get from your other patients. Right now we have no way to categorize and treat really crazy prisoners. We don't know whether to send them to the penitentiary or the Larned State Hospital."

Crawford considered cases with social malfeasants as totally different challenges. It would be another professional test in his career. "Thank you for thinking of me, Chief. I would be delighted to serve in the jail clinic."

Doctor Crawford had been practicing his skills in the Saint Michael Hospital jail clinic for a couple of years when a document came directly from Judge William Dodge. It involved a young boy who faced life imprisonment without the chance of a parole.

CHAPTER 30

H oratio Gilhooly was taken from his cell in the Sedgwick County Jail by a guard and told to bring his meager belongings with him. He was then handcuffed and ushered down to the alley in back of the jail. A patrol car with two policemen was waiting for him. The passenger cop took Horatio's bundle from the jail guard, then checked the kid's handcuffs and put him the back seat. The driver cop drove them down the alley to Broadway and turned north.

Although neither one of the policemen spoke to Horatio, the boy figured rightly that he was on his way to the hospital that Attorney Carl Banter had told him about. He sat back and enjoyed the outdoor sights that swept past the car window as they traveled toward their destination. It was calming after being in a small cell for such a long time.

The police car reached 11th Street and was steered left toward Saint Michael's Hospital. The trip ended at the rear of the building. From there, Horatio was taken out of the car and led to a door. The entry was opened with a key and the trio entered a small room where an elevator was located. The two cops ushered him into the conveyance and the three went up four stories. The doors opened to reveal the bars of a large door. Behind that was a row of six beds. The nearest prisoner had his left arm in a cast while another was sitting up in bed reading a newspaper.

A police male nurse sitting at a desk looked up. "Hi, guys."

One of the policemen spoke, "We got another customer for you, Larry."

"Yeah, I got his paperwork here."

Larry Mason was a large muscular man who had been a combat medic in the European Theater of the War. He stood up and uncuffed Horatio. The cops left as Mason took the new prisoner down a row of beds. "Okay, kid. This is where you're gonna live while you're visiting us."

"Yes, sir," Horatio said.

"The latrine and shower room are through that door over there," Mason said. "Your meals will be brought in here. You'll be getting better chow than you had at the jailhouse downtown. The meals here come from the hospital kitchen."

"Thank you, sir."

"Don't thank me, kid. Thank the Wichita taxpayers."

Mason went back to his desk and Horatio sat his bundle of belongings on the bed. The prisoner reading the newspaper stopped to watch him. "You look pretty healthy, kid. What brings you in here?"

"I'm going to have a mental examination."

"Let me give you a hint. Act real crazy. The funny farm is better'n the slammer anytime."

"I'll remember that," Horatio said. He looked around and saw a table and shelf. There was reading material of books, magazines and the two Wichita newspapers on it. "Is it okay to read those things?"

The prisoner showed him the newspaper he had been scanning. "Whataya think I'm doing with this. The Salvation Army brings in reading material every Saturday morning." He paused. "By the way my handle is Wilson."

Horatio sat down on his bed. "My name's Gilhooly. What are you in here for?"

"I've been sentenced to a three-to-five stretch for stealing a car. Then I had to have my appendix taken out. As soon as I recover, I'll be heading up to Lansing."

"My two brothers were in Lansing a few years back."

Wilson was interested. "I thought the name Gilhooly was familiar. Burglary, right?"

"I don't recall," Horatio said, not wanting to talk anymore. "Well, I think I'll go over and get something to read."

He walked across the room and stood in front of the table studying the offerings. He saw an interesting looking book titled *Great Expectations* by a novelist named Charles Dickens. He picked it up and walked back to his bed.

Wilson gave out a low whistle. "You're a real smart guy, ain't you?"

———

DWAYNE SPENT THREE DAYS IN HUTCHINSON testifying at the trials of Shorty Barlow, Jeb Clemens, Katy Clemens, George Carson, and Wanda Carson. The other criminals at Four Corners had gotten away to parts unknown. Their cases had been turned over to the F.B.I.

Now, as he parked the K.B.I. car in front of the apartment house, he let out a comforting sigh. He walked to the building and went upstairs. Donna Sue had been waiting for him when he entered the apartment. "I'm glad you're back, sweetie. You sit down on the sofa and I'll get your favorite drink."

He settled himself and waited until she brought him the whiskey. "I think I'll go to bed early."

"You can't, honey. You have to go to a wedding this evening."

Dwayne frowned. "Who the hell is getting married?"

"Maybelle will be the blushing bride. She and her boyfriend got their marriage license this morning and are going to get married at the chapel in the Salvation Army building."

"What boyfriend?"

"You remember hearing things about Johnny Lewis. He drives a truck for the Whitaker Laundry. Don't forget that Maybelle was fired from her job when poor Tommy was killed. She couldn't stay at the Randall Hotel any longer. And the couple didn't want to break the law by living together without being married."

Dwayne controlled his temper. "Oh, hell! I'll go then. I suppose you're the maid of honor."

"No. Her friend Sally Duncan is going to do that. And Sally's boyfriend is going to be the best man. He's a friend of the groom." Donna Sue hesitated. "Uh...there's another reason for the marriage, honey. It's kind of a long story."

Dwayne frowned. "Cut the story short, Donna Sue!"

"Carl Banter called the office to speak to you a few days ago and I told him you were out of town."

"I haven't heard from him in a long time. What did he want?"

"It seems that the youngest Gilhooly boy has a chance to be declared innocent," Donna Sue informed him.

"How the hell can that be?"

"Horatio Gilhooly was forced to go with his brothers on their crime sprees."

"Goddamn it! What the—"

Donna Sue interrupted him. "Carl Banter wanted you for a character witness."

"No way!"

"The boy is eighteen years old and has suffered cruel treatment from his brothers all his life," Donna Sue explained. "They beat him for the least reason. And his mother pulled him out of school when he finished the eighth grade. Horatio was a straight A student and it broke his heart that he couldn't continue his studies."

Dwayne calmed down. "Mmm, maybe there's something to this."

"Judge William Dodge has declared that Horatio will be given a psychiatric examination. They've already transferred him from the Sedgwick County Jail to Saint Michael's Hospital. He'll be tested by a Doctor Crawford."

"That's good," Dwayne said. "I'm acquainted with the shrink." He finished off his whiskey. "I guess I better take a shower if I'm gonna go to a wedding."

———

THE MARRIAGE BETWEEN JOHNNY LEWIS AND Maybelle Gilhooly went smoothly in the Salvation Army's chapel. There was the bride and groom, Dwayne and Donna Sue, Sally Duncan and Alf Jackson who was her new boyfriend and the best man. He, like Johnny Lewis, drove delivery trucks for the Whitaker's Laundry.

Dwayne felt melancholy during the ceremony. It brought him sad memories of his mother's suffering so many years ago. He smothered the grief as the Salvation Army minister conducted the nuptials. Johnny took the ring from Alf and slipped it on Maybelle's finger. The young couple was now man and wife.

Suddenly Dwayne wanted to cheer up. "Let's all go over to the Stockyards Restaurant for some steak dinners. It's all on me."

"Hey, Dwayne, give us girls a chance to pretty up," Donna Sue said.

"You're already pretty," Dwayne said. He looked over at Johnny. "Ain't they, Johnny?"

"They couldn't get more prettier."

Donna Sue laughed. "Listen to that. Johnny's going to be a good husband."

"Okay," Dwayne said. "You can follow me."

Each couple was in a car as they headed for the steakhouse. Maybelle snuggled up to Johnny giddy with happiness. Now she and Johnny were married and there was a good chance that Horatio could live with them after he got his freedom.

Dwayne and Donna Sue were in the Nash station wagon while the youngsters followed in Johnny's car. They parked side by side in the parking lot. The small group entered the restaurant and were seated at a large circular table in the back of the dining room. When their waiter came to the table, Dwayne ordered beer for himself and the other two men while Donna Sue ordered red wine for the three women.

The conversation was light and humorous. Dwayne and Johnny told some funny witticisms about being in the army while the others made fun of the supervisors in Whitaker's Laundry.

The evening was pleasant for the diners. The steaks, rolls, salads and potatoes were delicious for all. After deserts of apple pie à la mode, the group left the restaurant making cheerful goodbyes as they walked to their cars.

Donna Sue looked at Dwayne. "What made you cheer up and invite everyone to the steakhouse?"

Dwayne shrugged. "I overheard Johnny and Alf talking about going to a drive-in movie tonight to celebrate. I though a wedding supper would be better."

"Dwayne Wheeler! Sometimes you really amaze me!"

CHAPTER 31

There was a section of Wichita called Eastborough. That location was where the wealthiest and most prominent of the citizenry lived. It was reached by driving east as far as the end of Douglas. From that location onward, the thoroughfare was Shady Lane.

All the homes were elegant mansions set back along curving residential streets that boasted beautiful shrubbery and trees. The posh people in those opulent dwellings were so wealthy that they had established a police department of their own that watched over them day and night. All of those well-paid hired burly rent-a-cops had been deeply vetted and were quick to keep the peace. Lawless intruders who sneaked into the community received a dressing down that was accompanied by hard punches to the face that result in bloody noses. Then they would call the Wichita police to come and arrest the bad guys.

The *crème de la crème* residents used a recreational area called the Prairie Wind Golf and Tennis Club. As well as golf and tennis, there was a gymnasium, an exemplary dining room, ball room and a small male-only club where members could conduct confidential business matters.

One of the wealthiest of the ritzy population was Doctor Durward Crawford. His mansion was super spacious with five bedrooms, six baths, a dining hall, a well-stocked kitchen and a swimming pool. Crawford, his wife Hilary and fifteen-year-old daughter Iona were serviced by two live-in maids, a cook and a chauffeur. That driver was only used by the wife and daughter. Crawford preferred to go about in his 1940 Mercedes-Benz 170S.

In spite of this luxury, the Crawford family was down-to-earth, practical and rather nice people. At that time the good doctor was busy preparing to examine a young prisoner in the jail part of Saint Michael's Hospital.

———————

THE TWO COUPLES, JOHNNY AND MAYBELLE Lewis along with Alf Jackson and Sally Duncan, had evolved into a small social group. Their activities were organized around two drive-in movies; these were the Pawnee at Pawnee and Broadway and the 54 Drive-In on East Kellogg. Every Saturday evening they would attend either one or the other. Johnny always drove while they left Alf's car parked in front of the Lewis family's house.

At the theater Johnny and Maybelle sat in the front seat of his '39 Dodge while Alf and Sally took the back. This arrangement was because Alf and Sally needed a place for some red hot necking. Alf was living with his brother-in-law and sister who were strict Baptists. They would never permit Alfie and Sally to fool around in his bedroom.

When the shows were over, the group would go to the

Armstrong Ice Cream Parlor. Then they would go back to Johnny and Maybelle's house where Alf's car was parked. He made good money driving for the laundry and was planning on saving up enough funds to purchase a tractor he could own to haul eight-wheel trucks for various transport businesses. He had to pinch pennies if he were to realize that plan. Sally lived in the Randall Hotel where men were not allowed on the women's floor. That meant he and Sally had to head for the woodsy Riverside Park for sexual intercourse. There was also a good number of other lovers scattered throughout the area.

———

LARRY MASON, THE MALE NURSE OF THE JAIL part of Saint Michael's hospital, looked up as the elevator door opened. Dr. Durward Crawford stepped out. "Hello, Larry. How's the world treating you?"

"I'm fit as a fiddle, Doc. I see you're here to take a good look at the Gilhooly kid."

"That's right. How has he been behaving?"

"Nice young guy," Mason answered. "He does a lot of reading and he gets along well with the other two prisoners." He stood up and took the keys off his desk. "C'mon, I'll let you in." He opened the sliding door of bars and shouted. "Gilhooly! You got company."

Horatio, sitting on his bed reading Hemingway's *For Whom the Bell Tolls*, looked up. When he saw the doctor walking up to him, he closed the book and got to his feet. "Yes, sir?"

The doctor held out his hand. "Hello, Horatio. I'm Doctor Crawford."

"How do you do?"

"I'm quite well, Horatio. How have you been doing?"

"Well, sir, this is better than the cells in the jailhouse."

"I suppose it is." He pointed to a door on the right side of the back wall. "Let's go back there and get to know each other."

After the doctor escorted him into the conference room, Horatio saw it was rather small with a chair on both sides of a single table. "Have a seat, Horatio. I see you're reading a Hemingway novel."

"Yes, sir."

"He's one of America's best writers."

Horatio nodded. "I'm sure he is."

The doctor walked around and placed his briefcase on the table, then sat down and opened it. "Who is your favorite author."

"Mark Twain. I can relate to his books *Tom Sawyer* and *Huckleberry Finn*."

"Well! You sound like a reader who goes after what he wants," Crawford said. After taking out a legal-size tablet, he unscrewed his fountainpen. "Tell me why you're in here, Horatio."

"I was stealing stuff out of farmhouses with my brothers."

"Tell me about those brothers."

Horatio spoke slowly and plainly. "Junior is twenty-five and Cornelius is twenty-two. Junior's real name is Timothy but Ma doesn't like him to use it, because that was our father's name. He ran off and we never heard from him again."

"Do you have any other siblings?"

"Yes, sir. Maybelle is my sister and I'm quite fond of her and she of me. She's the oldest of all of us."

"Are you fond of your two brothers?"

Horatio remembered what to say. "Well, sir, they are

quite mean to me. They punch me a lot and boss me around. A lot of that is because I didn't like to steal."

"I see," Dr. Crawford said. "The file that was prepared for me indicates that you left school after you completed the eighth grade."

"My ma couldn't let me go to high school. I was quite upset about that. My brothers never reached the eighth grade but the two quit school when they reached sixteen years of age. Kansas law allows that."

"It seems you were very sad about having to curtail your education."

"Oh, yes sir!" He paused and took a breath. "I cried a lot about that. My teacher came to our house and tried to get Ma to let me go back and at least finish high school. But Ma told her to get out of the house."

At that point the interview continued with Horatio's living conditions, the lack of friends outside of his home and other parts of his lifestyle. The last subject was about his mother and it was another sad part of his life. The interview ended with more about his mistreatment from his brothers.

"Ma plans for us when we go out to rob. She told us to take things that bring a lot of money."

"What sorts of things?"

"Well, kitchen utensils mostly. And nice go-to-meeting clothes."

"What did you do with those stolen items?" Dr. Crawford asked. He already knew the answer to that question from the charges against the Gilhooly boys. This was to see if Horatio would continue being honest with him.

"My brothers took loot to an out-of-the-way place in Reno County. Ma did all the selling to an old man named Shorty."

"Where in Reno County was this, Horatio?"

"I've been there but I don't know the actual location. We have to cross a bridge over a creek to reach the place."

Dr. Crawford put the tablet back into his briefcase. "This is enough for our first session. I'll be back tomorrow." He stood up. "Are you familiar with I.Q. tests, Horatio?"

"I never had one, but I know what they're for."

"Well, you'll be getting one tomorrow so prepare yourself for a long session."

CHAPTER 32

Dr. Durward Crawford presented himself in the Saint Michael Hospital jail early on the morning of Horatio's scheduled I.Q. test. The male nurse Larry Mason opened the barred door for him.

"Good morning, Doc. You'll find the kid over there by his favorite place here. That would be going to the book table."

Horatio heard his name mentioned and turned his attention from *A Farewell to Arms* by Hemingway. "Hello, Doctor."

"Hello to you, Horatio. I see you have another Hemingway novel."

"Yes, sir. You made him an interesting writer for me."

"Good!" the doctor said. "Are you ready for the I.Q. test?"

"I've been thinking about that since you left yesterday," Horatio replied. "I'm interested in seeing if I'm smart or dumb."

"Not to worry," the doctor said as they walked toward

the rear of the ward. "You're certainly not dumb, believe me."

When they went inside the small conference room Horatio sat down while Dr. Crawford pulled the questionnaire out of his briefcase. He held it up. "This is a test I designed after much study and trials. I call it the Crawford Problematic Intelligence Quotient Examination."

"That sounds pretty complicated to me."

"There are no wrong answers, Horatio. It's divided into three parts, i.e. Visual, Spatial and Logical. The visual part involves pictures and design."

"That's interesting," Horatio said.

"It can be," Dr. Crawford said. "The second part is Spatial which is the study of an area of multiple intelligences. In other words, you will visualize with your mind's eyes. And lastly is Logical which is a testing of formal argument."

"Is this a long test, Doctor Crawford?"

"It will take you approximately two hours or more," Dr. Crawford said handing the I.Q. packet over to him. "So! There are pencils in here for you to use. Lay the test out and start working, young man. As for me, I am going downstairs to the hospital's snack shop for breakfast."

———

CARL BANTER SAT IN THE CONFERENCE ROOM OF Wichita's women's jail. Judge William Dodge had assigned him to represent Lilly Gilhooly the day before. This was the first time he would meet her and he was curious about this modern Ma Barker. The door opened and a matron ushered Lilly over to the table.

The matron set her down on the chair opposite

Banter. "Mind your manners. This is your attorney so try to remember he's on your side." With that advice expressed, the woman went to the far wall and took a seat.

"How do you do, Mrs. Gilhooly," Banter said.

"How are my boys?"

"Let's talk about you first, Mrs. Gilhooly."

"No! No! I want to know how they're getting along!"

"I'm going to have to ask you to calm down," Banter stated sharply. "That's the only way you'll be doing Horatio a big favor." He lowered his voice so the matron couldn't hear him. "So listen up. Your two older sons are sure to be found guilty of second degree murder. There's no doubt about them going to the penitentiary for life. And that will mean without any chance of a parole. But if you do as I tell you, there will be a chance for Horatio to get a much better deal. The judge is interested in him."

"So what? He'll end up going to Lansing Penitentiary anyway!"

"Mrs. Gilhooly, I wasn't just talking through my hat when I told you to calm down." He leaned forward. "If you don't behave and follow my instructions, Horatio will be in prison with your other sons. Is that what you want?"

Lilly took a deep breath. "I don't trust you or that judge. Our kind don't get no mercy."

"Maybe you and those other sons of yours don't. But Horatio has got a chance, understand? Now are you ready to listen to me?"

Lilly spoke softly. "Well...Horatio is my favorite."

"Okay. Your sons Timothy and Cornelius have told us that they were rough on Horatio. They said they whipped him with their leather belts at times."

"They never done that!"

"Shut up!" Banter hissed. "By revealing their cruelty

toward him which includes being forced to burglarize houses, indicates he was doing the crimes against his will. Also, you forced Horatio to quit school after his eighth grade. His principal came to your house to ask you to let him return to his studies. She told you the boy should stay in school because of his good grades."

"I told the bitch to get off our property," Lilly whispered defensively.

"That's good. It adds to Horatio's suffering."

"Wait a minute! His sister Maybelle and her boyfriend came to the house not too long ago. They said they wanted to take him away, and I let 'em."

"That was because he was your favorite son where the murder was committed. I'm sure you want him to live with his sister and her boyfriend. Isn't that right?"

Lilly took a deep breath. "Yeah."

"That's another good break for Horatio."

Lilly slipped into thought. Banter, as a veteran attorney, could see that she was mulling things over.

Five minutes passed, and she finally spoke in a normal tone of voice. "Yes! Horatio's brothers were always cruel to him. And yes! I pulled him out of school and I let Maybelle take him away from me."

"That's fine, Mrs. Gilhooly," Banter said. "Now let's see what can be done for you."

Lilly laughed sarcastically. "I ain't got a chance."

"I believe you were deserted by your husband and left to raise four kids."

"That son of a bitch Tim did exactly that," she said. "There was no way in hell for me to make enough money to feed us. Eventually the kids would have been put on the county and split up."

"Then you came up with the idea of burglary, right?"

"Yeah. The boys got perty good at it. Junior and

Cornelius went with Horatio after I tuck him out from school."

"That means you made them commit those crimes to keep the family together."

"O'course...wait a minute! I think I see where you're going with that."

"That's it, Mrs. Gilhooly. Now listen to me very carefully."

Banter began laying out how he was going to defend her and her boys.

———

Doctor Durward Crawford finished his breakfast in Saint Michael's Hospital café and checked his watch. He saw that Horatio had another hour to go on the I.Q. test. He took the elevator back up to the jail. When he stepped out he was startled to see that Horatio was on his bed reading *A Farewell to Arms*.

The doctor turned to Larry Mason the male nurse. "How long has he been there?"

"About fifteen or twenty minutes."

"Unlock the door, Larry."

Horatio heard him and turned his head. "Oh! Hi, Doctor Crawford."

The doctor gritted his teeth. "Why didn't you finish that I.Q. test?"

"I did finish it. I left it in the room."

Dr. Crawford strode angrily across the ward. The test was laid neatly on the table. He picked it up and opened the packet. He thumbed through it and noticed the Visual part was finished...that the Spatial was finished and also the Logical. The whole thing was completed.

He walked over to Horatio's bed. "You finished that test in under an hour?"

"Yes, sir. I found it very interesting."

"Fine, Horatio," he said. "Well...I guess I'll take it with me now to analyze."

"Okay, Doctor," Horatio said, turning back to his reading.

CHAPTER 33

A ttorney Carl Banter, District Attorney Wyatt Cunningham, Dr. Durward Crawford and Judge William Dodge were seated around the table in the latter's chamber. Banter was worried. If D.A. Cunningham learned that the physical batterings by the Gilhooly brothers on Horatio were a sham, the kid would end up with a life sentence.

The judge opened the conference, stating, "Carl, you're the first."

"Thanks, Your Honor," the attorney said. "My defendants Timothy Gilhooly and Cornelius Gilhooly wish to plead guilty and will accept the court's sentence of life without parole."

The D.A. spoke up. "Unfortunately I cannot accept that without the third Gilhooly being sentenced with his brothers."

Judge Dodge looked over at Banter. "What did you find out, Carl?"

"A hell of a lot, Bill. Horatio Gilhooly was forced to aid in the crimes by beatings and cruel treatment from his brothers. He was also pulled out of school to aid and abet those brothers and his mother against his will. He was forced to participate in their crimes."

"Your Honor," Cunningham said, "I would like for Doctor Crawford to report his conclusion of Horatio Gilhooly."

"What are your findings, Doctor?" the judge asked.

Dr. Crawford cleared his throat. "The young man was helpless because of his physical and mental mistreatment. Also, he had a strong unfortunate loyalty toward his mother Lilly even though she took him out of school. This weighed heavily on the boy because of his devotion to education. The principal of the school in question visited the house to plead with Mrs. Gilhooly to allow Horatio to continue his education. Lilly ordered her off the Gilhooly property."

D.A. Cunningham laughed. "He was going to a country school and getting a third class education. Why no—"

"Excuse me," Dr. Crawford interrupted. "I administered an I.Q. test as the last part of my examination. Perhaps country schools do not measure up to those in the city, but he scored 135 on the test. That, Mr. Cunningham, means he is a genius. Period."

The judge let out a whistle of admiration. "I can tell you right now that I'm going to give that young man a break."

Cunningham was alarmed. "Jack the Ripper was also a very intelligent fellow. He killed all those women and got away with it. To this day, no one has the slightest idea who he was."

Carl Banter let out a chuckle. "There's a hell of a lot of difference between a genius Kansas schoolboy and a nineteenth century insane killer, Bob." He turned to the judge. "Horatio has a sister named Maybelle living here in Wichita with her husband. He drives a delivery truck for Whitaker Laundry where Maybelle worked before the Gilhoolys were publicized. Horatio had a job as janitor in that same place before he was arrested. Maybelle and Horatio are very close to each other."

Cunningham interrupted. "I wouldn't be surprised if that truck-driving husband has a criminal record."

"Maybelle and her husband Johnny Lewis live in a modest duplex near Hillside and Victor Street," Banter said. He put his briefcase on the table and opened it. "I've looked up Johnny Lewis. He is twenty-three years of age and is an Army veteran with an honorable discharge."

"That's all very interesting, Carl," the judge said. "I want you to visit Maybelle and Johnny Lewis and see if they are capable of taking care of Horatio while we continue investigating the boy."

———

IT WAS EARLY THAT EVENING AS CARL BANTER drove his car from his office in the Central Building toward the house of Mr. and Mrs. Johnny Lewis. He was in a good mood. When he called the Lewis number Maybelle answered and said she and her husband would be happy to discuss her brother.

Banter turned east onto Victor Street and slowed down as he scanned the neighborhood for the Lewis address. The lawyer found it and parked in front of the duplex. He hurriedly picked up his briefcase and walked briskly to the front door. A ring on the bell was answered by Johnny Lewis with Maybelle beside him.

"You must be Horatio's lawyer. Come in. I'm Johnny. Johnny Lewis. And this is my wife Maybelle."

"Glad to meet you two young people. My name is Carl Banter and I am Horatio's attorney."

"Make yourself to home," Maybelle said. "You can sit in that easy chair and me and Johnny will sit on the sofa. Would you like some coffee, Mister Banter? I've got some fresh brewed."

"Why yes, Mrs. Lewis. That would be nice indeed."

Banter opened his briefcase and pulled out Horatio's records. Maybelle came back and set the cup of coffee on the side table by the lawyer. After she settled beside Johnny, the attorney began his presentation.

"I know something that's going to please you. Judge William Dodge who is going to oversee Horatio's case is quite happy about him. In fact, he is going to let him leave the jail and move in with you two. If you want him to."

"Oh!" Maybelle uttered. "Yes! Yes!"

Johnny took Maybelle's hand and grinned at Banter. "He lived here with us before he got put in the slammer, Mister Banter. He was a good brother-in-law as far as I was concerned. And he did quite well as a janitor while he worked in the laundry."

"That's fine," Banter said. "I'll see to getting his release. That'll be in a couple of days. Now to get to other business. Horatio was taken from his downtown cell and transported to the Saint Michael Hospital. He—"

Maybelle interrupted. "Is he sick?"

"No, Mrs. Lewis. He was transferred there for a physical examination and also an I.Q. test. That—"

Maybelle interrupted again. "What's an I.Q. test?"

Johnny broke in. "It's a test to see how smart a guy is, sweetie. They give 'em in the Army."

"That's right," Banter said. "And I'm going to surprise you with the fact that Horatio scored 135 points. That means he's a genius."

"Is that good?" Maybelle asked.

"Yes," Banter said. "That is *very* good...now let's get down to what could be called a plan to get Horatio back into the outside world." He looked at Maybelle. "Your two brothers are in this same scheme. I've told the judge that they have been horribly vicious to Horatio and—"

Maybelle spoke up angrily. "They ain't never done nothing really mean to Horatio!"

Johnny took her hand. "It's a lie on purpose that your brothers have harassed Horatio."

Maybelle didn't calm down. "Why are they lying? Junior and Cornelius are going to be worse off!"

"Maybelle," Banter said in a soft voice, "Junior and Cornelius couldn't be treated worse unless it was hanging. However, they are going to receive life sentences with no chances of parole. Understand? They can say they mistreated Horatio to make him take part in the burglaries against his will."

The frown on Maybelle's face turned to a look of surprise. "I see! If they think he didn't want to steal but was told to or get beat up then they *made* him do it."

Banter wasn't quite sure what she meant, so he took a chance. "Yes, Maybelle. That's exactly what we're going to do. The judge will give him a suspended sentence and he'll be free to do as he pleases. And you must never, *never*, *never*, tell anybody else about how we got Horatio out of prison."

"And he can come here to live with me and Johnny?" Maybelle asked.

"Not only that, but the Wichita Board of Education has teachers that go to certain students' homes to give them lessons," Banter said. "And Horatio can begin in the level of the ninth grade. Judge Dodge is fixing that up."

Maybelle sobbed in happiness. "Horatio is going to be

so full of joy. I can't wait to see him walk through our front door."

"There is one more thing but I don't think it will bother you and Johnny," Banter said. "He will not be allowed to get a job. In other words, you two will have to support him for the next three years. He will be free to go out as long as one of you are with him. He can go to movies, restaurants, parks and all that. Just remember he can't be alone. The two of you will act as his escort."

"Don't worry," Johnny said. "We've already learned to get along with him." He laughed. "He's a good cook, too."

CHAPTER 34

W hile Dwayne was gone as a K.B.I. agent Donna Sue made some plans about their future detective business. She typed up a list of ideas and made some calls to find the right commercial sales companies in Wichita.

After three days on the phone, she found an outfit that fit the bill. It was Peavy Commercial Real Estate Incorporated, an efficient business run by a married couple. Harold and Rachel Peavy came to Wichita from Chicago. The stiff competition their small outfit battled against in that metropolis offered nothing but ultimately bankruptcy. They decided to find a better place where they could make real money. The Peavys did some heavy research for what they were looking for in business reports. Eventually their efforts came across information on Wichita, Kansas. They liked what they read in a pamphlet about the location. The municipality offered a welcome for new businesses, especially in real estate.

Harold and Rachel visited Wichita in 1938 and found Sedgwick County a good market. Aircraft manufacturing was in high swing with Boeing, Cessna, Beech along with a growth in commerce. The couple arrived and wasted no time in establishing their business. They had a couple of stumbles but eventually the Peavy Commercial Real Estate Incorporated was well established with a building on Harry Street across from the Meadowlark Golf Course.

———

DONNA SUE CALLED PEAVY COMMERCIAL REAL Estate and made an appointment for one o'clock. After a quick lunch she gathered up the paperwork and headed for the real estate office. Sue noticed all the cars parked in the employment area were expensive models. She considered that a good omen. She got out of the Nash Station Wagon and walked toward the one-story light blue building in front of her. She stopped and studied it, noticing there was a curious combination of extravagance and simplicity about it.

Donna Sue shifted the briefcase she carried and walked through the front door. The lobby was small with a receptionist behind a modish desk metal desk. "May I help you, ma'am?"

"Yes. I have an appointment with Mister Ed Bronson. My name is Wheeler."

The receptionist picked up an inner-connection phone and spoke into the mouthpiece. "Mister Bronson, you have a caller in the lobby."

Within a minute Ed Bronson appeared. "Hello, Mrs. Wheeler. How are you today?"

"Just fine."

"We certainly appreciate your interest in us. Let's go

inside and see what we can do for you." He was a good-looking cheerful man with a head of thick blond hair.

Bronson escorted Donna Sue down a corridor that had illustrations on the wall of many of the company's sales. He stopped at a door and opened it to let her in first. She noticed the walls in the room were filled with photographs of historic Wichita that went back to the days of cattle drives and gun fighters. Bronson pulled out a chair for her then walked around the table to the other side.

"Well, Mrs. Wheeler, what can Peavy Commercial Real Estate and I do for you?"

"My husband and I have a private detective business that has been doing quite well for a long time," Donna said, giving him a business card. "We think it's about time to move our business from the WKH Building to larger quarters."

"That wouldn't be Dwayne Wheeler, would it?" he said, then chuckled. "Of course! You're Mrs. Wheeler."

"I am the administrator and bookkeeper of our agency."

"I've read a lot about your cases in the newspapers," Bronson said with a pleased grin. "And that includes news broadcasts on the radio." He took a fountain pen out of an inside coat pocket. "I don't believe I've ever sold a detective agency. Tell me what I'd have to find for you."

"We need a small building that could be turned into an office. That would also include a receptionist lobby and office area. One restroom would be enough. If there's no parking on the streets, then the property would have to have space for customer's cars."

"I see," Bronson said, writing on the pad. "Anything else?"

"This going to sound a little strange. The location has

to be in a neighborhood where the agency wouldn't stand out too much. Most of our customers prefer confidentiality."

"Of course!" he said cheerfully. "If you wouldn't mind I would like to introduce you to our owners. I believe this is the first detective customers we will be serving."

They went out into the corridor and down to where a very efficient executive secretary was stationed. Bronson spoke up, "Miss Temple, I would like to speak to the chiefs."

"Of course," Miss Temple said pushing a button on an intercom. "Mister Bronson would like a word, please."

A voice came out of the interior. "Certainly."

Bronson opened the door and let Donna Sue enter first. She saw two desks facing each other. The one on the left had a placard reading HAROLD PEAVY and the one on the right read RACHEL PEAVY. On the wall between was a large map of Sedgwick County.

Mr. Peavy showed a friendly smile. "Yes, Ed?"

"This is Mrs. Wheeler who has just signed up for us," Bronson said. "I thought you'd want to know her husband is a well-known detective in Wichita. That would be Dwayne Wheeler."

"Of course!" Peavy said. "And what are we going to do for the Wheelers?"

"We are going to find them a new office. Right now they're in the WKH Building downtown and want to find more space."

Mrs. Peavy showed a friendly smile. "I take it you're working with your husband, Mrs. Wheeler."

Donna Sue liked her right off. "Yes. I'm the administrator. I've also gone out with my husband on some of his capers. That is to say his jobs."

"That sounds exciting!" Mrs. Peavy exclaimed.

After a few more comments, the Peavys thanked her for becoming a client. Bronson led Donna Sue out of the office, taking her back to the lobby. "I'll be getting in touch with you, Mrs. Wheeler."

She walked out to the parking lot and Bronson turned around to go back into the building. The receptionist stopped him. "Mister Peavy wants to see you."

"Then I better go see what Mister Peavy wants, right?"

He walked rapidly back through the corridor. When he reached the secretary, she said, "Mister Peavy says for you to go straight in." He stepped inside the executive office. "Yes, sir?"

Peavy leaned back in his chair. "Ed, we want you to turn all your attention to the Wheeler Agency. And bring us written reports on where you've been taking them at the end of every day."

Bronson was taken aback by the unusual instructions. "Yes, sir!"

———

DWAYNE RETURNED TO WICHITA A DAY EARLY. He walked into the office, took a deep breath and gave Donna Sue a quick kiss. "Well, it's started."

"What started?"

"This Gilhooly caper is going to be wrapped up. Carl Banter is taking the two Gilhooly goons before Judge Dodge to confess their crimes. That pair of killers requested a quick transfer from the Wichita jail to the good ol' Larned Penitentiary. I can't blame them. Our local lockup isn't exactly luxurious. And it looks like Ma Gilhooly over in the ladies' lockup is going to have a life sentence but without the murder tacked on to it. Judge Dodge was lenient because she was an old lady who might be paroled to an old folks home to end her days."

"I see," Donna Sue said. "Well, here's a surprise for you. Horatio Gilhooly has been handed over to his sister and brother-in-law. Judge Dodge arranged quite a program for him. He can't leave the Lewis house unless he is with one or both of them. He will be taking home studies from the Wichita Board of Education. It seems he is a genius and when he earns a high school diploma there will be a scholarship waiting for him at Wichita University. Judge Dodge arranged for that, too."

"A Gilhooly is a genius?"

"He certainly is. The jail psychiatrist gave him an I.Q. test. And he's turned out to be a genius." Donna Sue paused for a moment. "And I have arranged for Peavy Commercial Real Estate to find us a new place."

"How did you describe what we wanted?"

"I specified a reception room and an office. And it must be in a neighborhood where we wouldn't attract too much attention."

"Way to go, sweetie! Now where's my Jack Daniels Sour Mash Whiskey?"

CHAPTER 35

It was a Monday midmorning when Ed Bronson pulled up his 1941 Chevrolet 4-door sedan in front of the Wheelers' apartment house. Dwayne and Donna Sue were waiting for him at the curb. Dwayne opened the back door for Donna Sue, then took the passenger seat next to Bronson.

Bronson eased back into the traffic, saying, "Mister Wheeler, I'm pleased to meet you. I'm Ed Bronson."

"My pleasure. My first name is Dwayne."

"All right, Dwayne. I have three places to show you this morning. I have your wants written down as Mrs. Wheeler dictated. If none of those catch your fancy, there are plenty of other places in Wichita proper."

Donna Sue said, "You can call me by my first name, too. It's Donna Sue...oh! That's two names, isn't it?"

Bronson chuckled. "Now we're just like family."

Their first introduction was out on East Douglas. This was a bookstore between three other businesses. When they reached the destination, the trio got out of the car, looked around at the neighborhood, then went to the door. Bronson took out the key for entrance. Dwayne and Donna Sue looked around the inside. The empty building had obviously been well cleaned and the size was perfect and had an area that would make a good lobby. They went in and walked around eyeing the interior.

"This looks pretty good, Ed," Dwayne said. "Let's see what else you've got."

They went back to the car and Bronson went up to Twenty-First Street that ran east and west just north of Wichita University. This was an older neighborhood with mixed homes and small businesses. Bronson pulled up in front of what was once a small notary public office and merchandizing. They went through a door into an excellent area for an office. Dwayne and Donna Sue also noted that there was not a lot of traffic going by. Bronson led them up to the door, unlocked it and stepped back.

Donna Sue expressed her opinion. "This also could also be made into a perfect detective office."

Dwayne nodded his agreement. "I like the ambience."

Donna Sue looked at him. "Where did you pick up the word *ambience*?"

"Mmm." He uttered. "I don't believe I know, love." He turned to Bronson. "You've really done well two times now, Ed. Let's see if you can show us that third perfect one."

"I'll do my best!" Bronson said. "I have another place on Harry Street. That's the same street Peavy Commercial Real Estate is on."

He drove back along Twenty-First Street to Hillside and turned south. Twenty minutes later he reached Harry Street and headed east a short way. Bronson turned into a what appeared to be a shopping center of sorts. There were two rows of one-story buildings with a third located crosswise on the end of the layout.

"I know this place," Dwayne said. "It has offices as spin-offs for both businesses and storage. Another good choice Ed!"

"And I thank you, Dwayne," Bronson said. "A man with a store in here had contacted Peavy Commercial Real Estate. I figured it would interest you two since there was not much activity in the area and it was out of sight."

He drove to the middle of the north row and stopped in front of a building. There were no windows except for one on the door. The glass was frosted opaque and couldn't be seen through. The structure's size was a narrow 180 feet by 540 feet. The latter measurement was the same for most of the buildings in the vicinity. A few others were wider.

"Let's see if it would suit you two as *perfecto*," Bronson said. He took out a key and stuck it in the lock with a twist. "*Entrez* as the French say."

Dwayne flipped on the light switch. The entry was a small lobby. It was a perfect place to put in a counter or a desk. A single doorway was to the left. "I could station myself out here," Donna Sue said.

Dwayne and Donna Sue went to the entrance door and stepped into an empty room.

Bronson followed, saying, "There's plenty of space for desks and file cabinets. A bathroom with a water fountain are on the wall at the back."

"We'll take it," Dwayne said.

"I have several other places to show you tomorrow," Bronson said.

"Nope. This is the one we want."

Donna Sue wasn't sure. "Let's look at some other places, Dwayne."

He looked at her. "This is one we *want*!"

Donna Sue sighed. "If you say so."

THREE DAYS LATER DWAYNE AND DONNA SUE signed all the papers and paid a thousand dollars for their new office. Dwayne drove out of the Peavy Commercial Real Estate Incorporated lot and headed west on Harry Street.

"I'm gonna show you something," he said.

"What're you gonna show me?"

"I'm gonna bring back memories of one of our first capers together," he said, turning into the spot where their new office was located. He came to a stop on the far side of the site.

Donna Sue asked, "What's this all about?"

"C'mon and get out."

He took her hand and walked past a small Chevy coupe to a door. There were closed venetian blinds in the large picture window. Dwayne turned his attention to the doorbell. He pushed the device twice, then gave a long three-start push followed by another quick two.

"Dwayne, what in the world are you doing?"

"It's a code."

The door opened and a woman appeared. She was a small slim brunette in her middle-years. "Well, for crying out loud, Dwayne! Where have you been hiding?"

She looked at Donna Sue. "Hello."

"Hello."

Dwayne spoke up. "You gals are Rachel Brooks and Donna Sue Wheeler whose name use to be Connors before she married me."

"Congratulations," Rachel said.

Dwayne turned to Donna Sue. "This office is for Wichita's number one call girl organization known as Venus Services. Rachel gets requests on her phone here from customers then sends out ladies of the evening to entertain the horny clientele."

Rachel looked over at Donna Sue. "I used to be a call girl but I was in a serious car crash that left my legs badly scarred. We working gals have to be as unblemished as angels even if the customers are overweight, sweating slobs. So I'm now on the telephone handling the get-togethers. I'm not complaining. My boss is a very nice lady named Mrs. Davis."

"I know her!" Donna Sue exclaimed.

"Well, we're neighbors now," Dwayne said. "We're over there on the other side setting up a private detective business." He changed the subject, looking at Donna Sue. "Do you two gals remember the time when Donna Sue here had to be hidden in Mrs. Davis' mansion because she was in danger from the Kansas City gang?"

"Was that you?" Rachel asked Donna Sue.

"Yes."

Mrs. Davis was a madam owning the Venus Services. The woman, once a star in silent movies, was fond of Dwayne because he had taken care of a couple of bothersome blackmailers for her. The lady let Donna Sue stay in her mansion north of the city for a couple of months in hiding from enemy gangsters. Eventually Donna Sue became friendly with a Miss Kathryn Carruthers who was Mrs. Davis' secretary. She taught Donna Sue how to type during the stay. She built up being able to type 80 words a minute. That gave her enough skill to leave hash-throwing at the Jayhawker Restaurant when it was safe for her to leave the mansion.

With ability in typing, Donna Sue began studying to be a stenographer. From there she worked her way up into the executive offices of a petroleum business called

Murchison Enterprises. This separation of Dwayne and Donna Sue ended their romance.

When Donna Sue's married boss wanted her for a mistress she refused and left the posh job to sink down to being a receptionist in a construction company. Dwayne had been called by the owner to trace his wife's whereabouts during the day. Dwayne found Donna Sue employed in that company's office. Short story: the couple got together again.

"Well," Dwayne said. "We're setting up an office here now. It's on the other side."

Donna Sue gave Rachel a hug. "Let's get together now and then."

———

THE NEXT MONTH FOR DWAYNE AND DONNA SUE was hectic and chaotic. They sold their old furniture and took money out of the doorjamb of the apartment to purchase brand new up-to-date desks and file cabinets and then have it all moved into the new office. There were mundane things to take care of like giving their new telephone number to Millie at the Reliable Answering Service, getting new business cards printed up, notifying others of their new location, getting the electricity turned on and some other bothersome chores. Dwayne finished it all up when he put a doorbell on the front door.

Finally, on a fresh Monday morning, Donna Sue brewed some coffee, and they sat down at their desks: Donna Sue in the reception area and Dwayne in the office. Within a few short minutes the phone rang.

Donna Sue answered, "Wheeler Detective Agency. Where may I direct your call?"

A Look At Book 6:

Wichita Déjà Vu

1950s Wichita, Kansas

When bail bondsman A.J. Kessler asks Private Detective Dwayne Wheeler to accompany him to a small town in western Kansas to capture an escapee, he never imagined being involved in a shoot-out that would end in one man's death.

Arrested by two U.S. treasury agents, who promise him freedom in return for his help, Dwayne is quickly released and thrown into his own personal hell as two young gangsters—with their minds set on getting even—make it their life's mission to hunt him down.

But when Dwayne is asked to join in on a secret South American government project, he realizes that his adventures have only just begun. Can Dwayne locate the east coast mafia... Or will he live in peril forever?

Wichita Déjà Vu is book six in a historical private eye series that follows Dwayne Wheeler—a tough and hardboiled detective.

AVAILABLE DECEMBER 2022

ABOUT THE AUTHOR

Patrick Andrews was born an Army Brat on January 14, 1936—his sister's arrival just two years later. His father was a paratrooper in the 82nd Airborne Division during World War II. His mother was a good army officer's wife, who, like several of her lady cousins, wrote short-stories and poems.

After the war, Patrick's father transferred into the Army Reserves, and they moved to Wichita, Kansas—where Patrick caught the scribbling bug. When Patrick got a job as a copy boy at the *Wichita Eagle* newspaper, he was ecstatic.

A few years later, Patrick got a yen to be a paratrooper. He enlisted in the Army and took basic training in Camp Chaffee, Arkansas, soon after being transferred to the 82nd Airborne Division in Fort Bragg. His career with the 82nd was rewarding—being promoted to sergeant and tasked with training cadets in West Point before retiring.

When Patrick read James Jones' *From Here to Eternity*, he appreciated the pride and struggling of soldiers. Soon after, he moved to San Diego, California and began writing and mailing manuscripts while working at a union typesetting company. He married and had one child, named William Patrick.

One pivotal night, Patrick was with a couple of his writing buddies, drinking scotch whiskey and playing at writing the *Sixgun Samurai* series. The next day, they drove up to Pinnacle Books in Los Angeles, where they walked out with a book deal. Patrick and his friends went on to write the series' twelve novels—which were also printed in the U.K. by Star Books, the paperback division of W.H. Allen & Co.

From then on, Patrick started writing and selling western, men's adventure, and military fiction. Years passed, and he had 24 published e-books with Piccadilly Publishing in the U.K.

Today, all six of Patrick's Wichita Detective books are getting another chance to see the light of day—with Rough Edges Press—and find refuge on a cozy shelf in Ocean Hills, California where Patrick and his beloved wife, Julie, live.